Eva Moves
the
Furniture

EVA MOVES THE FURNITURE

Margot Livesey

Marget Livesey

Henry Holt and Company   New York

Henry Holt and Company, LLC
Publishers since 1866
115 West 18th Street
New York, New York 10011

Henry Holt ® is a registered trademark of
Henry Holt and Company, LLC.

Library of Congress Cataloging-in-Publication Data

Livesey, Margot.
    Eva moves the furniture : a novel / Margot Livesey—1st ed.
       p.   c.m.
    ISBN 0-8050-6801-5 (hb)
     1. Imaginary companions—Fiction. 2. Maternal deprivation—Fiction. 3. Young
women—Fiction. 4. Scotland—Fiction. I. Title.

PR9199.3.L563 E84 2001
813'.54—dc21   00-143895

Henry Holt books are available for special
promotions and premiums.
For details contact:
Director, Special Markets.

First Edition 2001

Designed by Paula Russell Szafranski

Printed in the United States of America

1   3   5   7   9   10   8   6   4   2

Part I

BALLINTYRE

1

In 1551 the Italian surgeon Fiorovanti was travelling in Africa when he came upon two men fighting a duel. The cause is unrecorded: a camel? a woman? While Fiorovanti stood watching, one man sliced off the other's nose. The fight continued, but the surgeon's attention was elsewhere. He retrieved the flesh from the sandy ground and rinsed it in urine. As soon as the fight ended, he accosted the owner—winner or loser, again we don't know—sewed the nose back on, applied balsam and bandages. The patient, convinced only that absurdity was being heaped upon his suffering, argued throughout these ministrations. But eight days later, when Fiorovanti removed the bandages, there was the man's face, once again whole.

I do not know when or where Fiorovanti was born, but I was born in 1920 in the lowlands of Scotland, outside the town of Troon, less than thirty miles north of Alloway, where Robert Burns lived. It is a mild-mannered part of the country. The fields are fertile and predictable, with foaming hawthorn hedges and woods of beech, chestnut, and birch. Even as a little girl I judged the landscape inferior to the one I knew from stories, the fierce, dour Highlands where my mother had spent her childhood. My father, who had never travelled north of Glasgow, felt the same. Into his accounts of her life he wove the old legends: stories of the valley where Agricola's lost legion held sway over the blue-faced Picts; of a glen, high in the Cromalt Hills, where the dead carded and spun wool, gathered honey, and made mead and no one could distinguish them from the living. You might think such tales would have been rendered counterfeit by the barrage at Ypres and Armentières, but in my childhood they were still common currency. Perhaps the weight of so many new dead could only be borne with the help of the old.

I arrived in the upstairs room at Ballintyre close to morning on a mild April day after a labour that lasted twenty-four hours. The midwife who attended my mother sat by the bed, knitting a cardigan for her nephew out of the slate-grey wool left over from the endless socks and scarves of the War. The soft clicking of her needles accompanied my mother's struggles.

The midwife turned two sleeves, the earth turned once, and my mother's cries ceased with almost shocking completeness. "There, Barbara," said the midwife, her forearms streaked with blood, "I knew you could do it. You have a lovely girl."

She held me out towards the bed.

"Closer," begged Barbara. Without her glasses the world wavered. Obediently the midwife stepped forward into the circle of light that fell around the oil lamp; Barbara extended a cautious hand. Only then, as she touched my skin, warm, damp, smoother than a rose petal, did her fears subside. She yawned.

The midwife smiled down approvingly. "That's the ticket. You take a wee nap while I show Mr. McEwen his daughter."

Crooked in her arm, I would like to think I gave some sign of protest at leaving Barbara—curled my toes or furrowed my brow—but the protests that are recorded came from elsewhere. We were almost at the door when an outburst of sound drew the midwife to the window. In the early morning light a flock of magpies was fighting in the apple tree. The tree was in full bloom, and as the birds tussled among the branches, the blossoms drifted down, like snow, onto the dark soil. With a harsh screech a bird flew away over the garden wall; one by one the others followed.

"What is it?" asked Barbara drowsily.

"Some magpies squabbling in the apple tree." The midwife leaned towards the glass, counting. "One, two . . . six," she declared.

"Six magpies? Are you certain?"

But already we had turned away again. "Take a nap," the midwife repeated from the door. "I'll be back in a trice."

She carried me down the narrow stair, scarcely wider than a tea tray, to the kitchen, where my father, David, had sat through the night, embroidering a cushion cover. Later he would show me the awkward fern that marked my advent. When the midwife opened the door, he leapt to his feet. The two of them gazed down at me, David blinking back his tears. "Eva," he said. "Welcome."

The midwife praised his choice of name and sent him to fetch more coal from the scullery. I was tucked into a dresser drawer beside the stove. They had a well-earned cup of tea. David paced back and forth, too excited to sit but sufficiently mindful to ask after the midwife's nephew; she described his engineering exams in detail.

When she had finished her tea, she carried a cup upstairs. How soon did she know that Barbara was not merely asleep? From my own experience, I suspect as soon as she opened the door. Illness has an aura; it hovers above the body. Whatever hope lingered would have been banished by the raspberry hue of Barbara's cheeks, the nickering of her breath.

The doctor took Barbara's pulse, listened to her chest, and shook his head. No penicillin in those days. The influenza was back, he said, and squeezed her hand in farewell.

Saint Cuthbert's churchyard already had two whole rows of graves marking the autumn of 1919. In one of my nursing books a map showed how the disease spread north, like oil creeping up a wick. It passed from Manchester to Bradford, Bradford to Newcastle, Newcastle to Berwick, and on up through Scotland until eventually cases were reported as far north as John o'Groats. My parents had survived unscathed until the morning of All Hallows', when Barbara fainted at the breakfast table. She was unconscious for four days and confined to bed for a month. Then she had seemed to recover—until I arrived.

One of Barbara's favourite stories, also one of mine, was "The Little Mermaid," and that is how I imagine her death that day. As the sun rose she passed back through her youth and childhood down to the sea. Deeper and deeper she dove, to where the king's daughters kept their gardens, and the fishes and sea horses greeted her like an old friend. Nothing could call her back, not my father's urgent voice at her bedside, not my cries, which rose in volleys from the drawer beside the stove. Perhaps the noise even sped her on her way; she had stayed only long enough to bring me into the world.

Some parts of this story are true in one way, some in another. Now that I too have worked, married, had a child, I bring to Barbara's life the details of my own. My birth, the visitation of the magpies, her abrupt decline: these oft-repeated tales took on the lustre of the much-polished, seldom-used mahogany table in the parlour.

The magpies were the midwife's story. When I was old enough to go shopping with Aunt Lily, we sometimes met her bicycling down the main street in Troon. She would stop, straddling her bike, to chat about her most recent delivery. If matters had gone well, she was full of banter. Failure made her sombre, and then the sight of me, a reminder of one, drew a windy sigh. "I never saw a woman fade as fast as Mrs. McEwen," she would say. "One minute I was showing her the baby, and the next she was gone. Just a slip of a lass."

"Barely twenty," Lily confirmed. "You did everything you could."

The midwife shook her head. "Maybe if I'd sent for the doctor when I saw the magpies. I'll always regret mentioning them. The last words she heard, poor lamb."

"You can't trust the birds," said Lily. "We saw three at the bottom of the lane this morning."

Together they repeated:

"One for sorrow, two for mirth,
Three for a wedding, four for a birth.
Five's a christening, six a dearth,
Seven's heaven, eight is hell.
And nine's the devil his ane sel'."

"I've no plans to get married," Lily went on. "And you don't see four at every birth, do you?"

"No," admitted the midwife. "Well, Eva looks bright as a button. Are you being a good girl?"

I mumbled a yes into the scratchy tweed of Lily's skirt. The midwife patted my head and pedalled off down the street.

Ballintyre had been our family's home ever since my grandparents rented the house from a local farmer. David and his two sisters were all born in that same upstairs room. Later, Violet married an Edinburgh greengrocer, and Lily moved to Glasgow in 1914 to be a secretary. But David had gone on living in the doughty stone house, first with their parents, then without them. At the age of forty-six, he had surprised everyone by up and marrying Barbara. When she died, after less than two years, he summoned Lily.

Lily wept as she read the telegram. Only the past summer she and Barbara had spent hours walking on the beach, gathering razor shells and discussing whether animals had souls and how Lily, recently enfranchised with other women over thirty, should cast her vote. They had joked about the long wait before Barbara could enter a polling booth. "Eleven years," Lily had said.

She never thought, as she packed an overnight bag and told her employer she needed a week's leave, that her own life too had been struck by lightning. But almost as soon as she crossed the threshold at Ballintyre and found David blinded by grief and every room shaken by my cries, the impossibility of departure became apparent. She telegrammed her employer for a second week's leave, and at the end of that she wrote two letters, one resigning from her job, another asking her landlady to pack her trunk and send it to Troon. Perhaps there was a third letter, a letter she never mentioned.

I wailed like a banshee until the night of the funeral. Then I seemed to decide that sorrow was the least of my tasks and gave my attention to eating and sleeping. Lily, a youngest child herself, had little experience of babies and her reminiscences of those early days were a catalogue of near disasters: the time she almost dropped me on the stove, the time a cat sneaked into my crib. "It's a wonder you survived your first year," she would say. "You led a charmed life."

The most serious occasion, though, an occasion in which her clumsiness played no part, she confided only after I had left home to study nursing in Glasgow. That spring I caught bronchitis, and Lily came to visit me in the infirmary. Perched on a chair beside my bed in the women's ward, she told me about the afternoon she'd been polishing the silver while I took a nap. She had sat at the kitchen table, rubbing the spoons until the bowls winked back at her; then she moved on to Barbara's hairbrush. She was working on the handle, a posy of embossed flowers, when she decided to check on me.

In the hallway she stopped, aghast. Sixteen steep wooden stairs led up to the bedrooms and there, within inches of the topmost stair, I lay. How Lily reached me, she never knew. In an instant she held me to her bosom. "Eva, my precious," she murmured. "My cherub."

When her terror receded, she carried me back to my room;

what she saw there made her startle all over again. My crib was in the corner, with the bars—here Lily gestured at the rails of the next bed—still in place. "Though what difference did that make," she added, "when you could barely sit up?"

I nodded, too hoarse to speak, and she turned to describing the church whist night. David too, when she'd told him, had merely dipped his head. Those early months he was like an automaton, lifeless as the young men sent back from France. If she had claimed to find me flying around the chimney, he would have nodded. He bicycled to and from his insurance office; he went to Saint Cuthbert's on Sunday; he did what Lily told him. Often in the middle of the night he slipped out of the house to visit Barbara's grave.

Shortly after Christmas he emerged from the underworld of mourning. One frosty evening he hurried into the kitchen and, without stopping even to remove his bicycle clips, took Lily's hands in his and thanked her.

So I came to consciousness in the company of these two middle-aged people—and a third, much younger. Barbara was dead but far from gone. On all sides were reminders that Ballintyre was still her home: a gauzy studio photograph above my bed, the back door she had painted scarlet, a curious hat stand in the hall which she'd rescued from Larch House, where she worked as a housemaid when she first came to Troon.

Lily and David spoke of her often, their tones suggesting that she was away on holiday and would, in her own good time, return. Indeed, as I followed Lily round the house, she sometimes addressed Barbara directly. "Why did you let David buy such a wee carpet sweeper?" she would say, or "How could you put up with this stingy washing line?"

In the evenings after supper, David took me onto his knee and told me stories. When Barbara was dying, he had clung to the notion that if he held her in his thoughts unwaveringly, if he did not allow himself for a moment to be distracted, his love would carry her to safety, like a raft across a dangerous river. Now he told me about her life with the same vivid concentration.

"Barbara grew up a hundred miles north of here in the valley of Glenaird. There was no town, like we have, only a famous boys' school and a big house, the Grange, where her father was a gamekeeper and her mother a housekeeper. Barbara divided her time between them according to season. In summer she accompanied her father on his rounds. In winter she helped indoors. Her mother said if she polished the brass door plates hard enough she would see her future husband."

"And she saw you," I said.

David laughed. "She saw someone with a moustache. She tried it once at Larch House, and the head housemaid gave her a terrible scolding."

"We went to Larch House today," I offered.

"That's right," said Lily. "On our way to the cobbler's."

Then it was time for another kind of story. David told me about a boy, born on the Isle of Skye, who wouldn't stop growing. He became a giant, famous for his strength and his bad temper. "He had very big white teeth," David said, clicking his own modest ones. "And people used to say, whenever a boy or girl disappeared, that Hamish had eaten them."

Later, as I climbed into bed, I was sure the giant was lurking in the garden, waiting to sink his teeth into me. If I opened the curtains, I would see him, towering over the apple tree, nose pressed to the glass. I clutched Lily's hand and babbled my fears.

"The giant is from long ago, Eva. We don't have giants now at Ballintyre, and if we did the Wrights' dogs would chase them away."

"Oh."

"There aren't any giants," Lily repeated. "Do you want to take out my earrings?" She bent down so I could reach her ears. While I fumbled the fine gold wires out of the mysterious holes, the giant tiptoed away.

By my fifth autumn I could walk the mile into town, and I joined David in his weekly visits to Barbara. On Saturday after lunch we picked a bunch of woody-stemmed chrysanthemums from the garden. Then we set off down the lane, David carrying the flowers, me skipping beside him. At the churchyard, he threw last week's blooms on the compost heap and filled the vase with fresh water from the rain barrel. Meanwhile I cleared away the fallen leaves. A copper beech grew near the door of the church, and week after week throughout the autumn, leaves blew across the graves. David set the chrysanthemums in front of the stone and reminded me that Barbara too had grown up visiting a churchyard. "Her sister, Elizabeth, died of polio," he said. "She was just fourteen, poor thing."

"Poor thing," I echoed cheerfully. Fourteen sounded old to me.

As he scraped a clump of moss off a corner of the stone, David described his first meeting with Barbara. He was waiting to see the optician—once again he had sat on his glasses—when the door of the inner office opened and a young woman stumbled out, almost falling over the threshold. David jumped up to help; glimpsing her damp cheeks, he proffered his handkerchief. In exchange Barbara confided her sorrows. Ever since she arrived in Troon, a few months ago, something had happened to her eyes. "I was always the first," she told him, "to spot the deer on the hills, the grouse in the heather. And now even the trees across the road are blurry." She had managed to conceal her condition until the previous Sunday, when her employer caught her squinting at the hymn board in church. "She was so upset," David said, patting the stone. "She was sure no one would ever talk to her again if she wore specs."

In my imagination the gravestone became a door. It swung open and there was Barbara, going about her daily business, polishing brasses, wearing her spectacles. She was nearby but inaccessible—rather like Aunt Violet, who lived in Edinburgh.

On our way to and from Saint Cuthbert's we passed Miss Mac-Gregor's school. I would stop and press my face to the gate, yearning to be among the boys and girls inside. Soon, David promised, and one afternoon, shortly after my sixth birthday, when Lily and I were making pie crusts at the kitchen table, he raised the subject.

"School," Lily exclaimed. "She's still a bairn."

"We went at her age."

Lily gave a snort and pressed down on the rolling pin so hard that a thin tongue of pastry hung over the edge of the table.

A few days later, though, she did produce a primer, and every morning, before the shopping, I sat making long rows of letters and numbers and reading about Percy, the bad chick. It was school I craved, not study, but by dint of threats and promises Lily drummed into me the three Rs. Soon I was adding my own postscript to the weekly letter to Violet: *Love Eva, xoxox.*

That summer was particularly fine, and I set up house for myself and Mary, my doll, under the red-currant bushes. When I had the rooms furnished, I fetched Lily. "Here's the kitchen," I said. "And here's your room. This is your bed."

"Very nice." Lily fingered a cluster of currants. "We'll soon be making the jam." She headed back to the kitchen.

A few minutes later a voice said, "What a cosy house."

A woman was peering through the branches. Everything about her shone as if she had been dipped in silver. Her hair was white as the swans I saw when David took me fishing, and she wore a white dress with little blue checks. "What's that?" she asked, pointing to an empty matchbox.

"That's the stove. And here's the pantry." I indicated a grassy niche lined with pebbles.

"Oh, you've made lots of preserves, like Aunt Lily."

I knew, of course, that they were only pebbles with grit clinging to them, but her understanding transformed them into rows of bottled plums and blackberries.

"I brought you something," said another voice. A girl with long braids joined the woman. She was seven or eight years older than me, with a rosy face and eyes the colour of bluebells. Her pinafore was hiked up so I could see her knees, dirty and grazed like my own. She handed me half a dozen acorns. "I thought they'd make good cups and saucers."

Both the woman and the girl looked familiar. Perhaps I had seen them at Saint Cuthbert's, or the Co-op? The sun had been shining all along and there was no wind, but now the day grew much warmer.

For a moment, with my two guests leaning through the doorway of my little house, I forgot to breathe. Everything was so clear and distinct that it seemed to leave no room for me. Then I thought I was only what Lily called overheated. I took off my cardigan and served them tea in the acorn cups; they sipped appreciatively.

Later, when I went indoors to wash for lunch, I told Lily, "The woman doesn't take sugar. But the girl likes two spoons."

"She must have a sweet tooth," said Lily. "Stand still. There's a twig in your hair."

Several weeks passed, enough time for me to have largely forgotten my visitors, before they came again. One morning Lily and I were on our way to gather the eggs when we heard the tinkle of the knife sharpener's bell in the lane, and she hurried off to give him the carving knife. Alone, clutching the egg bowl, I wandered down the cinder path towards the henhouse. At that age waiting, even briefly, made me feel as if I had been cut free of my moorings and was slowly drifting away.

"Why don't you go in and get the eggs? Think how surprised Lily would be."

The girl, in her blue pinafore, was swinging on the lowest branch of the apple tree. "I dare you," she said, dropping to the ground and darting around the side of the house.

What a good idea. There was the knotted door, the latch, well within my reach. I stepped inside and, setting the empty bowl on the straw, shut the door.

Lily treated the hens with businesslike contempt, and in her company I found it easy to do the same. "Move, chookie," I would say, and put my hand into the nest. Now, alone in the small hut, the nine hens grew larger and fiercer by the second. "Go away," I whispered.

Something warm brushed my leg. "Aunt Lily!" I cried. But the thick air swallowed my voice.

Jemima, the black hen, began to push forward.

"Shoo, shoo. Off you go."

The woman stood beside me, the silvery woman, clapping her hands. "Come on, Eva. Let's get the eggs."

I felt as I had beneath the red-currant bushes, suddenly squeezed and breathless. "Come on," she said again.

She held the bowl for me while I went from nest to nest, and I noticed she had to stoop to avoid hitting the cobwebby roof, whereas Lily could stand upright with ease. "See?" she said, at the last nest. "You don't need to be scared of the hens." She placed the bowl in my hands.

Before I could thank her, the sound of footsteps made me glance towards the door. By the time I looked back, the woman was gone. I could not have said how. Did she melt through the walls, crawl out of the hatch by which the hens came and went? Between one moment and the next she simply disappeared.

"Clever girl," Lily said. "You got the eggs all by yourself."

"No. The woman helped me."

"That was kind. Next time maybe she can give you a hand to tidy your room." She took the bowl and ushered me out of the hen-house.

2

I am not sure now how long it took me to realise that the woman and the girl were different from our other neighbours. They appeared and disappeared mysteriously, they seemed to have no home, they would not answer simple questions: Do you like dogs? What are your names? "Don't ask," they said. "We're your companions." And usually I obeyed. The real difference, though, was not their reticence—most grown-ups were unforthcoming—but their invisibility. Several months passed, however, before this became apparent. They seldom visited when Lily and David were around, and in the beginning I was misled by idle remarks about tidying my room, having a sweet tooth.

Sometimes I wonder what would have happened if, on that first day beneath the red-currant bushes, I had fled screaming to summon Lily's adult scepticism without delay. But I doubt even she could have saved me. In my mind there was already much confusion between two categories commonly held to be opposites: the living and the dead. As for a third category, the ghosts in my storybooks were filmy, insubstantial beings who did not graze their knees or chase hens. The companions did not seem to fit into that group either; they existed in their own peculiar dimension.

The ambiguity was easier to contain because I never spoke of them aloud. When our Sunday school teacher explained that Jews did not utter the name Jehovah, I understood at once. I knew that feeling of leaving a blank, of missing a beat. If I could, even now, I would refer to them by a streak of colour, a note of music: the girl and the woman, blue and silver, D sharp and middle C.

Finally, the autumn after my seventh birthday, I set out for Miss MacGregor's with my stiff new satchel. I was afraid I would be the class dunce, starting two years late, but thanks to the mornings at the kitchen table, I turned out to be well ahead of the other pupils. After a few days my heart no longer thudded as I swung through the playground gate. Instead I discovered a new emotion: loneliness.

So far children had been a novelty in my life. Our nearest neighbours, the Wrights at the farm, had three grown sons, and there were no other families within easy walking distance. I had not felt the lack. Now, although my classmates welcomed me to their games of hopscotch and tag, I craved a particular friend. At first I pinned my hopes on Jessie Todd, with whom I shared a desk in the third row. She copied my work shamelessly, and I was careful to keep my slate in view.

Every afternoon began with spelling. Miss MacGregor came

down from the dais and paced the aisles between the desks. "Onion. Suppose. Abrupt. Pigeon," she enunciated, at measured intervals. One day, while we were wrestling with *argument,* she plucked Jessie out of her seat and marched her to the front of the room. "Jessie Todd," she announced, "has been cheating. You all know what cheating is, don't you?"

Hands went up. "It's copying," said the minister's son.

"It's stealing what doesn't belong to you," said the mole catcher's daughter in the front row. Jessie, her face red as a cockerel's comb, glared.

"Why is it wrong to let someone copy your work?" demanded Miss MacGregor.

She was staring straight at me, but I kept my eyes fixed on my desk, where someone had carved H E L L deep into the wood.

Ian Hunter waved his hand. "It's helping someone else to sin," he said. There were suppressed giggles. Ian—his father kept the forge—was the cheekiest boy in the school, always in trouble for scrapping in the playground or not doing his homework.

For two days Jessie refused to speak to me. Then, during the seven-times table, I sensed her, once again, squinting in my direction. I leaned back and edged my slate closer. Sharing my work was infinitely preferable to being ignored.

My longing for a friend was sharpened by Shona and Florence, with whom I sometimes walked part of the way home. Shona, Dr. Pyper's daughter, was plump and chatty, while Flo, whose father ran the Co-op, was thin and quiet. They lived next door to each other, near Saint Cuthbert's, and were unlikely best friends. When I accompanied them, Shona would entertain us with a stream of anecdotes about her father's patients. "And guess what?" she would say, and whisper the crucial information in Flo's ear. I counted chimney-pots, or sparrows, anything to prevent their guessing how much I minded.

Usually, however, I walked home alone, and then I summoned Jo and Beth from *Little Women,* Katy from *What Katy Did*, Curdie from *The Princess and the Goblin*. I could travel the whole distance from Miss MacGregor's to Ballintyre without registering a single detail of the landscape. But when the girl came to meet me, as she sometimes did beyond the forge, she needed neither speech nor gesture to get my attention; her presence thickened the air, as if light bent slightly around her. We would pick dandelion clocks and look for birds' nests. Or we played pirates, jumping over the puddles to escape capture.

Now that I was closer to her in age, she seemed to enjoy my company, but I had mixed feelings about hers. She did not have the same constraints as I did—to be home on time, to stay clean—and she bit her nails, a habit Lily had scolded me out of. Besides, I never knew what she would do next. One moment she could be wonder-fully sweet, showing me a thrush's nest or a strange purple mush-room, and the next, for no apparent reason, bad-tempered. Once, when I said I didn't like porridge, she shoved me in the ditch, muddying my shoes and pinafore, so that Lily threw up her hands at the sight of me. "Good grief, Eva. Were you playing with the pigs?"

Such encounters only deepened my desire for a real friend, one with whom I could share secrets but who was not, herself, a secret.

As the years passed, I became convinced that everything would change when I started grammar school. The red brick building with its separate entrances for girls and boys contained my new life, just waiting for me to come and claim it. I would be chosen first at games, given the lead in the school play, have tea parties every Saturday. And the companions? They would simply disappear. I would outgrow them, like my old pinafores which Lily turned into dusters.

On the first day of term I was hurrying down the lane in my new uniform when the woman stepped from beneath an ash tree. During those years she came much less often than the girl, so her appearance that morning, when even a second's delay seemed fatal, was especially hard to bear. Nor did I want that curious, uneasy feeling she usually brought in her wake. But there was no help for it; she fell in beside me. "So you're off to the grammar school," she said. "Are you excited?"

"Yes. I'll be doing French and Latin and there are all kinds of clubs."

"French was my favourite subject. *Je vais, tu vas, il va, elle va.* One year I wrote my Christmas cards in French. No one knew what to make of them." She laughed.

"What does *je vais* mean?"

" 'I am going.' Right now, though, I think the word for what we're doing is *dépêcher. Nous nous dépêchons.* We are hurrying."

We reached the water trough. From town came the sound of a bell chiming. The woman cocked her head. "It's only eight-thirty. Stop a minute."

Reluctantly I turned to face her and found myself caught in her deep-set eyes. At the time I would not have known how to describe their colour. Since then, I have seen that melting grey often in the eyes of babies—it seldom lasts. "Don't worry," she said. "You'll do fine."

She straightened my tie and headed through an open gate into a field. When there were no interruptions, she and the girl came and went like ordinary people. I watched her move away, her raincoat blending with the dun-coloured stubble, her hair shining. As I continued towards town, I discovered she had taken some part of my anxiety with her.

That afternoon Lily made scones for tea, but I couldn't stop talking long enough to eat. "There are maps all round the classroom. Miss Robinson asked us what we wanted to be when we grew up. I said an explorer." For my twelfth birthday, David had given me a book called *Great Scottish Explorers*.

"An explorer?" Lily shook her head. "What did you learn?"

"We each had to recite our favourite poem. I did 'To Autumn.' Miss Robinson said it was beautiful. I'm sitting next to Catherine Grant. She chose a poem by Keats too, the one about the sedge withering on the lake."

"Have another scone," said Lily. "I don't think I know Catherine. She's not in the Sunday school, is she?"

"No. Her family just moved to Troon this summer. She's awfully tall and she smells nice, like lavender." Jessie had always had a grubby smell.

"Eva, you know it's rude to talk about how people smell."

I continued to study Catherine in sly glances. At morning break she seldom joined in the games. I would see her loitering near the doorway, a heronlike figure in her grey pinafore. Such solitude might have made her seem an outcast, but there was a poise about Catherine; she had chosen to be alone and could choose otherwise.

Twice a week Mr. Waugh, the bluff red-faced minister, came to the grammar school to teach Scripture. In late September we read the Book of Job. All the disasters visited on the unfortunate Job, Mr. Waugh explained, were the will of God.

Catherine raised her hand. "Was it God's will," she said, "that so many soldiers were killed in France?"

Her naked phrasing sent a shock through the room. We said the men lost their lives or laid them down. Animals were killed. Even Mr. Waugh looked unnerved. "No, that wasn't God's will. It was man's."

"But if God is omnipotent," Catherine persisted, "why did He let it happen?"

I could feel her emotions radiating across the desk, though I could not name them. Was it grief that tormented her? Fury?

Mr. Waugh studied the Bible on his desk as if the answer might be hidden there. Finally he said, "One of the hardest tasks of a Christian's life is to accept that suffering is visited upon the virtuous. Almost all of us have lost someone. We console ourselves by remembering that our loved ones are safe with God."

My eyes filled. SAFE WITH GOD was the inscription on Barbara's stone. Years later, during another war, patients would ask me Catherine's question. Why does the sun shine upon the just and the unjust? Why does suffering lead to more suffering? I was no more convincing than Mr. Waugh, but at least I was not, simultaneously, defending my profession.

That afternoon, as I shelled the broad beans, I told Lily what had happened. Poor child, she said. Since I last mentioned Catherine, she had made it her business to find out about the Grants. While I nudged the beans from their furry niches, she explained that my deskmate was an orphan. Her father had never recovered from being gassed at Neuve-Chapelle; he had died three years ago, followed a month later by her mother. Now Catherine lived with her grandparents.

Next day I eyed her with even greater interest. I knew a number of children like myself, who did not have the full complement of parents, but to be an outright orphan was altogether more momentous. Several times she met my glance, and when school was over she followed me to the cloakroom. "It's my birthday on Saturday," she said. "My grandmother said I could invite someone to tea. Would you like to come?"

"Yes, please." Then I caught myself. "I'll have to ask my aunt."

I rushed home, full of plans. Only when I stepped into the kitchen and saw Lily at the ironing board, frowning over a pleated skirt, did I suddenly remember that the previous summer she had refused to let me have tea with the cowman's daughter. I decided to wait until she came to kiss me good night, always the best time to ask a favour, and meanwhile to be especially helpful. But as I was laying the table for supper, she said, "You're so quiet, Eva. Did the cat steal your tongue?" And before I knew what I was doing, I had blurted out the invitation.

"Can I go?"

Lily sprinkled water on one of David's shirts. "May I. Is it a special occasion?"

"Her birthday."

"In that case"—she pushed the iron over a sleeve—"I don't see why not. What will you give her?"

At once my pleasure was eclipsed by this difficult question. None of the usual gifts, ribbons, scrapbooks, toilet water, handkerchiefs, seemed like fitting ambassadors of friendship to Catherine. After two days of brooding, on Saturday morning in Calder's gift shop I finally bought a china milkmaid, eight inches high with a brimming pail of milk. The instant I got home, I showed her to Lily. "Do you like her?" I said.

"She's lovely." Lily bent to look more closely. "Look at her frock. And you can see each eyelash. How much did she cost?"

"Two shillings."

"Oh, Eva, that's a lot to spend on someone you hardly know."

I blushed. It was indeed twice as much as I had spent on Lily's last birthday present.

"There," she said. "I didn't mean to scold. It's very generous of you. I'm sure Catherine will be pleased."

After lunch I put on my best brown velveteen and set out, the box cradled in my arms. As I passed the Wrights' farm, I pictured the afternoon to come. Catherine would take me up to her bedroom. We would talk about being orphans, and I could contribute Barbara. I was nearly at the forge when I had an amazing thought. I could tell Catherine about the companions. Perhaps she might even be able to see them.

I was so startled, I stopped in my tracks. That the companions were invisible to Lily and David had become a fact of life. Now I realised I had never tried to introduce them to anyone else. I stood motionless, imagining the three of us—Catherine, myself, and the girl—playing together, making up stories and having adventures, until the clanging of the blacksmith's hammer roused me. I began to walk with increasing swiftness towards the town.

Catherine answered the door wearing a dark green dress which made her look more like a tree than a bird. She did not seem to notice the box, and I was too shy to hand it over directly. While she hung up my coat, I set it on the hall table. In the dining room, Mrs.

Grant was waiting to meet me. She was nothing like my idea of a grandmother. Her curly hair was the colour of a new penny and her lips were scarlet. Lily called women who used makeup Jezebels, but I was thrilled.

At tea Mrs. Grant made me sit on her right and insisted on serving me first. She asked about Lily and David, what was happening at the Women's Institute, whether David's office was busy. Across the table Catherine asked questions of her own. Did I ever ride Mr. Wright's cart horse? No. If I could visit any country I liked, where would it be? The Congo.

To my surprise there was no cake. Indeed, neither Catherine nor her grandmother mentioned her birthday. Could I have misunderstood? When tea was over Catherine took me not to her bedroom but to the back garden. After the rambling sprawl of Ballintyre, the square of paving stones surrounded by straggly flower beds seemed pitifully small. The only object of interest was a birdbath standing in the middle of the square.

Catherine lifted a twig out of the bowl; it was almost full of water from the recent rain. "What shall we do?" she said. "It's hard to play games with just two."

"I have a friend." I watched her pale hands moving over the bowl. "Maybe we could—"

A loud splash finished my sentence. Catherine screamed. I leapt forward.

In the bowl lay a stone the size of an apple. Raising my eyes, I saw the girl sitting on the wall at the end of the garden. Beneath her hard stare the distance shrank until I could have counted the freckles on her nose, eight of them, and the loose hairs pulling out of her braids. She stuck out her tongue and slid down the far side of the wall.

"Cripes," muttered Catherine.

Had she seen the girl, I wondered, but she was wiping her face with the skirt of her green dress. "Are you hurt?" I asked.

"Stupid! Why did you do that?" Her hair was dripping and her bodice patterned with dark stains.

"I didn't do anything." Instinctively, I stepped back. "It's only water. I'll get a towel."

She pointed to the stone. "I suppose a ghost threw this?"

The following year when Isobel taught me hockey, she often chided me for procrastination. "You have to tackle the minute they get the ball, not wait for a better chance." That afternoon, in Catherine's garden, I recognised my chance and was afraid. My earlier fantasies had fled. All I could imagine was her calling me daft. Or worse. Speechless, I gazed at the incriminating stone.

She led the way indoors and, with a quick parting nod, disappeared upstairs. On the hall table lay the forgotten milkmaid. I longed to reclaim her, but how on earth would I explain to Lily? I let myself out of the house and started to run through the gloomy streets towards Ballintyre.

On Monday, to my surprise, Catherine smiled as we took our seats. At break she thanked me for the milkmaid. "She's lovely. I put her next to my bed."

I fidgeted my feet back and forth in the gravel.

"I still don't understand," she continued, "why you threw the stone. I didn't even see you pick it up."

She was looking at me, not hostile but curious; again I let the occasion pass. I muttered something about an accident and hurried to join the other girls playing Lady Queen Anne beneath the chestnut tree. Shona Pyper stood in the centre, bouncing the ball, while the circle chanted:

> *"Lady Queen Anne she sits in her stand,*
> *And a pair of green gloves upon her hand,*
> *As white as a lily, as fair as a swan,*
> *The fairest lady in a' the land;*
> *Come smell my lily, come smell my rose;*
> *Which of the maidens do you choose?"*

"I choose Eva," called Shona.

As I took my place inside the circle, I felt Catherine watching from across the playground. All my daydreams were gone and I was terrified to think that she had nearly seen the girl. At home it was easy to overlook the strangeness of my situation. But in Catherine's garden I had understood that the presence of the companions in my life was like a hidden deformity: ugly, mysterious, and incomprehensible. If my schoolmates found out, they would never choose me.

3

Samuel told me the story of Fiorovanti the summer after we met. "And, abracadabra," he concluded, "plastic surgery. Must have looked like hell, but better than nothing."

He pointed towards his own unremarkable nose and raised his glass. We were in the pub, the White Hart, and most of the other customers were women from a nearby munitions factory, still in their overalls and kerchiefs. In fact Samuel probably didn't say, "Abracadabra, plastic surgery." He almost always used the term *re-constructive*, although before the war he had done his share of society women. "I can picture the whole scene," he said. "The two chaps quarreling over some trifle and old Fiorovanti waiting to have a go. Then the patient complaining nonstop until the bandages came off."

Across the table, I watched him flex his hands. I had seen other surgeons make this gesture, as if to reassure themselves; yes, it was still there, the suppleness, the steadiness. In the silly novels Lily read, the doctors had elegant musician's hands, but Samuel's were more like a plumber's. "Pound of sausages," he would joke, flinging his pudgy fingers down on the counter. Still, he had a reputation for making the neatest stitches in the infirmary. When I saw him at work in the operating theatre, I was amazed at the patience with which he would close an incision, attach a graft.

"And is that why you became a surgeon?" I asked.

"You mean, I learned about Fiorovanti at my mother's knee and decided to pick up a scalpel? Heavens, no. I wanted to be a pilot, then an archaeologist." He smiled a little sadly, as if envying his younger, carefree self.

"I used to want to fly," I said, trying to cheer him up. "So what happened?"

"My father. He said I could always fly later but I must study first. And visiting Hadrian's Wall cured me of archaeology. Everything was so hypothetical. The guide would point to a pile of stones and say maybe this was the bathroom, or perhaps they kept their spears here. Nobody seemed to know the answers."

"Out on the town again, doctor?"

"Ethel!" Samuel jumped up, nearly toppling the table, to pump the hand of a barrel-shaped woman dressed in factory overalls. "Eva, this is one of my prize patients. Ethel Donaldson. Nurse McEwen. Have you time for a drink?" he asked, pulling out a chair.

"Love to," said Ethel.

And that was how all our early meetings ended, with an interruption, so that soon I came to hate what I most admired about Samuel, his kindness. It spilled out, like air or rain, getting into everything, everyone, and drawing people to him. Even at our most intimate moments, I felt one of a crowd.

For a while after the disaster with Catherine, I tried to avoid the companions, but my loneliness was like the slow gas bubbling up from the pond in the woods, poisoning even the sweetest of days. How could I turn away those two who wanted to be my friends when no one else did? And they, as if they took my forgiveness for granted, sent what I thought of as their shadows. Later, at the infirmary, I overheard a couple of nurses talking about poltergeists, but whether that was the nature of these odd gusts and tremors that shook the curtains and moved the furniture I cannot say. Their connection with the companions seemed capricious, like a broom with dust or an umbrella with rain.

At first I doubted my eyes and ears. They came as I was falling asleep; in the half-dark I would glimpse a chair rocking, hear the wardrobe door creaking. Just my stupid imagination, I thought. By now I had learned to condemn the dense daydreams of childhood in which teachers still sometimes caught me ensnared. But in the morning I would wake to see the chair on its side, the wardrobe door open wide.

One afternoon, when David and I came home from visiting Barbara, Lily was making pancakes. Usually this treat indicated good humour. Today, however, she frowned and beckoned me to the stove. "Didn't you tell me you'd tidied your room?"

"This morning."

"Well, it's not what I call tidy. There are books everywhere. Your hairbrush was in the middle of the floor. Really, Eva." As she listed my misdemeanours, the pancakes bubbled. Lily flipped them, one by one.

From the top of the sixteen stairs, I could see my school atlas lying in the doorway of my room. The flesh of my arms rose in a thorny mixture of fear and rage. "Why do you do this?" I asked.

I bent to pick up the atlas and found it open to the map of France. *Dépêchez-vous*, I thought.

That winter groups of shabbily dressed men loitered outside the labour exchange; a number of shops closed; the windows of Larch House were boarded up. At tea David claimed the government had forgotten there were people north of Newcastle. "The whole of Scotland could starve," he said, "for all they care."

"Nonsense," said Lily. "The king was up at Balmoral in August. Eva, have another biscuit."

I did, grumpily. Although she often scolded me for having my head in the clouds, Lily herself, I'd begun to understand, was on awkward terms with reality. All kinds of topics—money, jobs, romance, religion, politics—were to be avoided, except in their most hygienic forms. When I asked an awkward question, she would purse her lips and bring the conversation back to my homework.

As the days grew shorter, the streets grew increasingly crowded, not just with men but whole families. After Christmas the weather turned bitterly cold. The sheep huddled together in the fields, and the birds were so hungry they tried to hop into the house. It had been freezing hard for a fortnight when one morning on the way to school a woman stepped in front of me with outstretched hand. "Excuse me, miss." She wore a man's jacket, the sleeves frayed and torn.

I backed away, shaking my head; I never had money during the week. Then, as she kept holding out her hand, I remembered my lunch. Hesitantly I offered the bag of sandwiches, and before I could change my mind she snatched it from me.

I was too shy to ask the other girls to share their food, and by the end of school my stomach was growling ferociously. I ran home, skipping over the icy puddles. At Ballintyre the kitchen was empty. I hurried to the bread bin. I was on my second slice when the back door opened and Lily appeared, the frozen sheets crackling in her arms. "What's this," she said, "an early tea?"

Between mouthfuls, I explained. I hadn't thought of my behaviour as praiseworthy, but neither had the possibility of blame occurred until Lily burst out, "Goodness, Eva, haven't I told you not to talk to strangers?"

"I didn't talk to her. She talked to me."

For years Lily had urged me to clean my plate by reminding me of the starving children of India; now she was obdurate. I was to walk with Shona and Flo. On no account was I to give away my lunch.

The following morning I took the long way round to catch up with the girls. Fortunately they welcomed my company. When we reached the corner of the terrace, Shona was dramatising the fishmonger's painful shingles. The beggar woman made no move, simply stood, watching us, empty-handed.

On Saturday on our way to the churchyard, I told David what had happened. "Poor woman," he said. "I'll give you a shilling for her. You must explain that you haven't any more. She can always get a meal at Saint Cuthbert's soup kitchen."

"What about Aunt Lily?"

"I'll talk to Lily. It's her duty to worry about you and I wouldn't want to contradict her, but you did right, Eva. The three of us are lucky. We should share what we have." His words hung in the air, little puffs of frozen breath, almost edible.

Barbara, he said, had done the same thing. Early in 1917, after two years at Larch House, she had gone to work in a munitions factory, a dangerous, noisy job she much preferred to housework. One week she gave her pay packet to a man who'd lost a leg in France. "I scolded her," said David, "like Lily scolded you, but I was proud. We went dancing that night at the Palais. I remember her hair smelled of explosives."

"What do explosives smell like?"

"Bitter, not unpleasant. I grew to like it." He smiled down at me. "Months after the war ended I could still smell the gunpowder when we waltzed together."

The first day I laid eyes on Samuel, he waltzed a sister around the ward. He had just examined the hands of a pilot and discovered two thirds of the graft healed, a result so pleasing that he'd seized the sister in her starchy uniform and begun to dance. I had stood there with the other doctors and nurses, staring, dumbfounded, while the patients stamped their feet or banged their lockers. It was September 1943, ten in the morning, and in my four years of nursing I had never seen such pandemonium.

On Monday the ragged woman was in her usual place. I handed her David's shilling and started to explain about the soup kitchen, but she was already trotting down the street. Later that day the temperature rose slightly. Walking home, I was caught in a stinging, cold rain, and by the time I reached Ballintyre my teeth were chattering. Lily sent me straight to bed. The next thing I knew, she and David were standing over me and the room was filled with the painful light of a new day. "Tell the doctor her temperature's over a hundred," Lily said, "and her glands are swollen. See if he can come right away."

David bent down. "Eva, darling, you'll feel better soon."

His pale, anxious face made me suddenly afraid. Only twenty-four hours ago I had played netball and conjugated Latin verbs. Now even getting out of bed was unimaginable. Was this how Barbara felt in her final hours? The corners of the room grew dim.

When Dr. Pyper arrived, he diagnosed measles.

"She doesn't have any spots," Lily protested.

"Give them time. Isobel Henderson was ill last week, and Grace O'Connor broke out yesterday."

At once I felt a little better. I was on a predictable path. As if by magic, spots did appear, and Lily became reassuringly brisk. The hardest part of being ill was not being allowed to read, but whenever possible David sat with me, telling stories. How Flora MacDonald saved Bonnie Prince Charlie by dressing him as her maid. How Barbara helped her father, the gamekeeper, set snares. And, my favourite, how she had rescued Keith Hanscombe from drowning.

Her first summer in Troon, Barbara went down to the shore every Sunday after church. She had grown up in an inland valley, and even though the beach was lined with barbed wire the sight of the sea fascinated her. One Sunday a boy slipped through the wire and, clambering on the rocks, fell in the water. Although she could not swim, Barbara had followed him onto the sand and waded out, thigh deep, to tow him back to shore. The boy was Keith Hanscombe and his mother, Marian, became Barbara's firm friend. She died in November 1917, an early victim of the flu epidemic, and her husband and two sons had moved away to Edinburgh.

While he spoke Lily had climbed the stairs. Time to sleep, she said, and they both kissed me good night. As soon as the door closed, the companions appeared. My illness made them gentle. On windy nights they quieted the windowpanes, and when the girl danced a Highland reel not a floorboard creaked. The night of the Mrs. Hanscombe story, she recited Burns's "To a Mouse" in a squeaky voice that made me giggle until the woman said, "That's enough. Lily's right. You should be asleep."

"Just five more minutes," the girl wheedled.

She produced a length of green wool and began to play cat's cradle. To my surprise she knew the difficult later stages of the game, which were the closely guarded secret of the older girls. A fortnight later when I returned to school, I enjoyed a brief wave of popularity. Then Shona asked where I had learned my new skills and a familiar anxiety pinched my pleasure.

Samuel told me about a philosopher, his name escapes me, who believed we are doomed to repetition; over and over we commit the same errors or those of our forebears. At the time the notion struck me as nonsensical. Now, sometimes, I wonder if my difficult birth is partly responsible for the trouble I've had crossing other thresholds. The first year of grammar school was as hard as, if not harder than, my first year at Miss MacGregor's; I was fourteen that spring, not

yet filled out, in Lily's phrase, and with no aptitude for the easy banter of friendship. As the weather improved, the crowds outside the
labour exchange dwindled. The farmers needed help, Mr. Wright
hired six men to clear his ditches, and work commenced on a new
town hall. Solitude made me a good student, and in July, when
school finished, I had come third in my class. But I was glad to return to the safety of my days with Lily.

Together we went for picnics, made an expedition to Glasgow,
gardened. When the red-currants ripened on the bushes where I
had once made a doll's house, Lily announced the jelly would be our
contribution to the church fete. We set aside a whole day for this
project, beginning after breakfast with stripping the bushes, then
cleaning the fruit, putting it on to boil, washing the jars, straining
the jelly. By the time David came home, I was writing the labels:
Red-currant jelly, August 1934.

After tea, Lily said she would do the washing-up and I fetched
my book and set off for my favourite willow tree. It grew on the
riverbank near the pool where David liked to fish, and in summer I
spent many hours lying in the leafy shade, reading or daydreaming.
That evening when I parted the branches, I discovered two men,
one dangling his feet in the river, the other propped against the tree.
I shrieked and dropped my book.

"Good evening, lassie," said the man leaning against the trunk.
He was older and, to my astonishment, wore a gold earring, like
Lily's only larger. The other was scarcely more than a boy, though
his stomach bulged beneath his torn shirt, and his teeth, when he
grinned, were sparse and walnut-coloured.

The older man lifted up the book and offered it to me.

"Thank you," I said. Once the first shock had passed, I was more embarrassed than scared.

The man's lips moved, but what emerged was a kind of grunt. The boy grinned again, stood up, and seized my arm.

For a second I was too startled to move. Then I twisted out of his grasp and ran. The boy followed, and in a hasty backward glance, I saw the man lumbering behind. I raced along the river's edge, dodging bracken and fallen branches. Just when I thought I had got clean away, my foot caught in a rabbit hole.

Even now, I have only a confused sense of what happened. The boy was upon me. Behind him the man loomed. And somehow, miraculously, they were gone. In their place were the companions. As they escorted me back to Ballintyre, they admonished me, almost in unison, not to tell anyone about the men.

The following afternoon Lily asked me to pick the peas while she attended a meeting of the church fete committee. The sky promised rain, purple clouds massed in the west, but nonetheless I worked slowly. Each pod helped to hold at bay the man's weird grunts, the boy's beery breath. I was only halfway down the second row when I heard Lily calling my name. Instantly my palms grew clammy. Why was she home so early? Had she somehow found out? I was still close enough to being a child to believe that adults could, if they chose, know everything about me.

In the kitchen Lily was leaning against the stove; she had not paused even to remove her brown felt hat. "Eva," she said, her voice rising, "there's something I have to ask you."

As I counted the knots in the floorboards, she explained how Mrs. Wright had stopped by the chemist's that morning and Mr. Cameron, the chemist, had told her about two men chasing a girl beside the river. He had been on the opposite bank, too far away to help or even see clearly. "You didn't meet any men, did you?" she asked. "Mr. Cameron said they looked like gypsies."

"No, Aunt Lily."

And to my amazement that was enough. Lily finally removed her hat and I stumbled back to the garden. The companions had saved me, but the price was high. As I finished the peas the first drops of rain fell. Liar, they whispered. Liar.

Perhaps it was that Saturday, perhaps a week later, when David asked me to visit the churchyard in his stead; he had a cold. Since meeting the gypsies I had stayed close to home. Now I pedalled down the lane as fast as possible. Every bush and tree was a potential hiding place from which the men might suddenly leap, grunting and laughing. But I saw no one save the Wright boys fixing a gate. They waved and I waved back.

Near the church, another kind of apprehension came over me. Although I had gone with David to visit Barbara's grave hundreds of times, it was different to go alone. When I pushed open the gate, the rusty groan of the hinges echoed my reluctance.

At some point during the preceding week the vase had blown over. As I bent to retrieve the cornflowers, I found myself reading the inscription. There was her name, Barbara Malcolm McEwen, the date of her birth, and the date of her death: my birthday. If

Barbara were alive, she would be my mother. It was a revelation. Like David and Lily, I always spoke of her by name.

"Mother," I said softly.

I stared at the stone, trying to shape my muddled thoughts into clean, neat prayers which could wing their way past the door of the gravestone into that other world where Barbara still kept house. I prayed to be like everyone else, or to have other people—even just one person—see the companions. Neither seemed remotely possible.

4

That autumn I grew listless, wept easily, slept fitfully. Lily even went so far as to take me to Dr. Pyper, who spoke of growing pains and prescribed a syrupy tonic which did little besides make me cough. What finally brought me back to myself was not medicine but theatre. The Saint Cuthbert's Dramatic Society was putting on *Saint Joan,* and David was playing an elderly soldier. By this time he was in his early sixties and Lily must have been over fifty, but like Barbara in her photographs they seemed ageless. I was the only one caught in the grip of time.

For two months David went to rehearsals every Friday, and on Saturday afternoons, as we walked to the churchyard, he recited his lines with gusto. On the night of the play, for once I was grateful for Lily's punctuality, which secured us seats in the front row. I read my book while she talked to the Waughs and the rest of the audience arrived. At last the lights went out and the curtains rose.

"There's George," whispered Lily. "Doesn't he look grand?"

I sat motionless. George was no longer the helpful stationmaster who gave us a hand with our shopping after a day in Glasgow. He was Robert, the squire, who adamantly refuses to receive Joan and ends by doing everything she wants. Joan herself was played by Maisie Proudfoot, daughter of the golf club secretary. A few weeks before, I had run into her on the number four fairway. While we chatted, a small clear drip wavered on the end of her nose. Now, dressed in armour, she swore to regular conversations with Saint Catherine and Saint Margaret; I leaned forward in my seat willing the wind to do her bidding. At the end of the play, Lily had to nudge me to applaud.

I was still in a daze when David emerged, carrying his tunic and spear, and the three of us started for home. Then, as we were passing the Bell and Bush, a remark of Lily's roused me. "Do you think," she said, "Joan really did hear voices?"

"I have no idea," said David. "She did manage to convince the most unlikely people to do what she wanted. I mean, suppose you'd gone to General Haig in 1916 and told him how to fight the war."

Lily laughed. " 'Miss McEwen, would you kindly lead Britain to victory?' "

I trailed after them, gazing at the gaslights, each with its misty halo. Of course we read stories in Sunday school about people who saw visions, but they were bearded men in remote places. Here was a girl, my age, who had lived not far away, in nearby France, and who had left her father's farm and everything she knew to lead an army into battle, all because of her voices. The companions did not tell me to take Edinburgh or save the king, but as I followed Lily and David up the lane, I was thrilled by the notion that I too might have some purpose.

On Saturday at the circulating library, I asked if there were more books like *Saint Joan.* "Do you mean other plays by Shaw or books about Saint Joan?" Miss Clapham demanded, pencil poised.

"Books about people like Joan."

"Ah, saints." She lowered her pencil, clearly disappointed that my request was so obvious, and directed me to Religion.

I examined a life of Joan's friend, Saint Catherine. The frontispiece showed Catherine about to be saved from the wheel. Later, despite being beheaded, she still retained her beatific smile. I moved on to Saint Margaret of Scotland, who initially seemed more promising, but after several paragraphs describing the hair shirt she always wore beneath her regal gowns, I let the book fall shut. I was due to meet Lily at the Co-op in a few minutes. Quickly I went to Literature and chose *King Solomon's Mines.*

Now I wonder why I looked in books rather than at the people around me. We had our share of strange folk in Troon. Mrs. Ord, who lived at the back of the grammar school, was believed to have the evil eye. And there was a story about a dairymaid, Agnes, who had drowned in the river going to meet her sweetheart. People said she walked at harvest time, the anniversary of her death. One afternoon on our way fishing, David showed me the spot where Barbara claimed to have met her. "Just here." He tapped the mossy parapet of the bridge. "She was wearing a mauve frock, very fetching, but all wrong for fording a river. That was what killed her, the weight of the water in the fabric."

He himself had never seen Agnes. Nor did I, though sometimes in August I remembered the story and looked for her. That Barbara's experience was similar to my own did not strike me until much later. But I did begin to hope that I was being prepared for some important task. Perhaps Mr. Wright's barn would catch fire and I would lead the animals to safety, or I would be warned that the roof of Saint Cuthbert's was about to collapse. For a month, in the hope of discerning some hidden agenda, I wrote down the details of every encounter with the companions in a diary which I hid on top of my wardrobe. The girl met me twice on the way home from school. And one afternoon, when Lily was at a church meeting, I found her in the kitchen holding a blue jug Barbara had bought. "We're not allowed to touch that!" I exclaimed.

She smiled, not pleasantly, and for a moment I was afraid she might dash the jug against the hearth. Then she put it back on the mantelpiece.

The woman came once when I was rearranging my room. I was moving the bed over to the window, and she asked if that wouldn't be rather draughty. Her words themselves were like a draught, and a leg of the bed promptly caught on a floorboard. As she headed for the door, she frowned in the direction of the wardrobe. I was so discouraged that I dragged the bed back to the corner.

That night, writing in my diary—*4:30 P.M. The woman visited. Came in without knocking. Queried my moving the bed. Grumpy*—it occurred to me that the companions were aware of my observations. What else could explain the look the woman had given the wardrobe? I glanced around. As if in answer, the rug rippled towards the door and a chair toppled to the ground. See? they seemed to say. You are never alone.

Quickly I sprang from the bed and returned the diary to its hiding place. At once the room grew still. As I took in the motionless rug, the fallen chair, I understood that my note-taking was a form of treachery.

The Saturday before Easter, Lily dispatched me to the garden to give the windows their annual spring cleaning. It was a bright, chilly day, and I found myself remembering the afternoon in Catherine's garden. Why had the girl, who seldom appeared in public, done so on that occasion? Suddenly I knew it was because I had been about to confide in Catherine. Whatever mission the companions had in mind for me, secrecy was imperative, not just from Lily and David but from everyone.

"Come on, slow coach," Lily mouthed through the window. I crumpled a wad of newspaper and began to rub the glass. Soon I could see my own reflection and behind me the apple tree trembling in the wind. And wasn't there a figure beneath the tree? Two figures? Wasn't the girl wearing her pinafore and the woman her raincoat? But when I turned around, the budding branches were empty.

I gave up on my investigation of saints and indeed forgot all about it until I met Father Wishart at the infirmary. I was on my second stint of night duty, and he had two parishioners on the ward: a pensioner with a broken hip and another I have forgotten. If the stern staff nurse was not around, Father Wishart often stopped for a cup of tea at the nurses' station. One evening he showed up even later than usual, his face pale and drawn, and told me he'd been keeping vigil at a deathbed. "May we all go like Nelly. A week ago she was playing bingo. Then a wee cold, and that was that." He smiled. "She was sure she saw Peter waiting for her at the pearly gates."

Everything conspired to make the occasion intimate: the small glow of the night lamp, the men sleeping around us. I offered more tea and asked if he had ever had a vision.

"I'm afraid I haven't been so blessed. Though I did once see the infirmary ghost, or at least I thought I did. He has the same name as you."

"Spelled differently," I said, and coaxed him into repeating the story. Sir William MacEwan had been a famous brain surgeon at the infirmary. A few years earlier a young man, a concert pianist, had come to consult him about the severe headaches which were threatening to ruin his career. After a brief examination, Sir William dismissed him as a hypochondriac. The young man left the surgery in tears and, on his way out of the building, tumbled down a flight of stairs to his death. Many called it suicide. At the funeral Sir William was seen to weep, and a couple of months later he died in his sleep. Since then several people had met him, pacing the corridor outside the operating theatre.

"He's meant to wring his hands in remorse," said Father Wishart, "but when I saw him he was walking along like anyone else, an elderly chap in a white coat. I only knew it was him because I glanced away, and when I looked back the corridor was empty." He gave a faint smile. "Och, I'm blethering, nurse. Probably I just need my eyes checked."

He drank some tea. A man groaned in his sleep. "Do you think," I said hesitantly, "Sir William is typical? I mean, do you think ghosts are always unhappy?"

"Goodness." Father Wishart stroked his chin. "I've never thought about it, but yes, I suppose so. The reasons the dead are restless, what drives them back to walk among the living, are usually sorrow and pain. If there are happy ghosts, they must be few and far between."

Before he could say more, the staff nurse's footsteps sounded in the hall. "Here she comes," whispered Father Wishart. "Thanks for the cuppa."

That morning when I went off duty, I walked over to the theatre. The corridor was busy with white-coated figures, preparing for the first operation of the day. They all seemed full of purpose. No one was wringing his hands.

I stopped writing in my diary and waited. Almost five weeks passed before I came upon the companions, leaning on the gate of a field, talking animatedly. As I approached, they fell silent and regarded me with the same expression of pointed enquiry that the older girls turned upon me when I interrupted them in the school cloakroom. I stopped a few yards away, blushing.

"I know I mustn't tell anyone about you."

"As if you could," the girl scoffed.

The woman, however, nodded nicely. She looked down at her hands and twisted the ring she wore back and forth. The next Sunday at church I noticed that the minister's wife wore a similar ring. Did the woman have a husband? Did the girl have parents? Even in the midst of my investigations, I never asked what happened to them when they left me. Twice at the infirmary I broke a thermometer, and I recall how the globules of mercury fled and scattered at my touch. That was what it felt like, to think of posing certain questions to the companions.

Presently the woman raised her head. "Why don't you join the hockey team?" she said.

"What do you mean?"

I didn't blink, I didn't turn away, but the gate was empty. I ran my palm along the top bar. The splintery wood was still warm.

At my first hockey practise a wiry girl with slightly protuberant brown eyes came over. "When the whistle blows," she said, "run forward and I'll pass you the ball. Then you pass it back to me." By some miracle I managed to do this, and though I missed every other shot in the game, Isobel Henderson befriended me. A few weeks later she invited me to the athletics club.

"I'm hopeless at games."

"Nonsense." Isobel grinned. "There are boys."

A chill wind blew across the sports field that Thursday, and while Isobel practised hurdling, I hopped from foot to foot. On the far side of the field were the promised boys. I spotted Ian Hunter among them; in the last year he had shot up. He caught me looking, and waved.

I raised my hand in reply; then, thinking better of the gesture, I pretended to straighten my pinafore. But Mr. Gillespie, the games master, had seen me. In his booming voice, he summoned me to the high jump. "We're starting at two foot six. Anyone can do that."

Reluctantly I joined five other girls. The only one I knew was Winifred, who had sung "Silent Night" at the Christmas carol service in a way that made Lily get out her handkerchief and reminisce about concerts in Glasgow. Now she soared over the bar with the same effortless grace. When my turn came, I jumped as if I were skipping a rope and almost proved Mr. Gillespie wrong.

The narrow escape roused my concentration. The bar was raised to two foot nine. This time I imitated the other girls, turning my body sideways and scissoring my legs.

At three foot six, two girls dropped out. It was my turn. I jumped and heard the clatter of the bar. "Try again," said Mr. Gillespie. "That was just your foot."

I ran towards the bar, and as I leapt, invisible hands lofted me into the air. I felt their touch, cold and firm, and briefly I forgot everything except that feeling. Then I was landing in the rough grass.

Surely people must have noticed? But Mr. Gillespie boomed, "Well done," and a couple of girls smiled.

There were only the two of us left: Winifred and I. The bar was raised. After two failures I was sure, on the third attempt, I cleared it, but again it clattered to the ground. Perhaps the spirits were safeguarding me from the ill effects of sudden success. Winifred also failed the jump, and Mr. Gillespie announced that was enough for this week.

I was tying my shoelaces when Isobel ran over. "What did I tell you? With some practise you could be okay. Do you want to come to my house for tea?"

"That would be grand." As I tightened my laces, I whispered my thanks into the wind.

5

For the next couple of years I had an unspoken truce with the companions. I did not try to pry into their nature and they in turn tolerated my friendship with Isobel and visited less often; months would pass without my seeing them. Meanwhile, in the world beyond Troon, great events were taking place. We celebrated Edward VIII's coronation with a pageant and dancing in the town hall. Less than a year later, I came home to find Lily crying at the kitchen table.

I dropped my satchel. "Aunt Lily, what's the matter?"

"That harpy," she sobbed. "She's bewitched him."

Gradually I pieced together that the man for whom I had danced a schottische was giving up the empire for an American woman, twice divorced. By the time David came home, Lily had dried her eyes and was as indignant as if Edward had jilted her. David shared her feelings. The king, he said, had betrayed a sacred trust.

Years later, in a cinema queue, I repeated these sentiments to Samuel. I've no memory of what film we were trying to see, or why the abdication came up, but his reply stays with me. "You people are such hypocrites," he said. "You put Shakespeare on a pedestal, yet you ignore everything he tells you. Anthony threw away an empire for love. Othello strangled his wife. What Edward did was nothing."

"Who are 'you people'?"

"Everyone who's not a bloody foreigner."

"But Samuel, you grew up in Edinburgh."

"No, I grew up a Jew." He traced something on his chest which later I guessed must have been the Star of David. "There are different ways to be a foreigner, Eva. Look at our patients. They're foreigners, until we fix them."

And I am too, I wanted to say, as the queue shuffled forward.

Shortly after the abdication, David brought home a wireless he'd ordered from Glasgow, and on a warm May afternoon the three of us listened to George VI's coronation. "These words are being spoken four hundred miles away," David marveled. Afterwards we walked to Saint Cuthbert's in our best clothes for a service of thanksgiving.

From then on David listened to the news most evenings. Sometimes I kept him company, but I found the prim English voices hard to follow, and the dark events of Europe seemed far away. While Samuel's cousins fled from Prague and Berlin, I was preoccupied with sports and the school play.

In July 1938 I finished school with a medal for high jumping and a third prize in English. The following Monday I began my first job, looking after the children of a Mrs. Nicholson, who was spending a month in Troon to convalesce in our sea air. The arrangements had been made by Aunt Violet (the two were neighbours in Edinburgh), and as I cycled into town I imagined my new employer wraithlike and consumptive. But the woman who jumped up to greet me in the lounge of the Station Hotel was plump-cheeked and ruddy with health, only a few years older than myself.

She led me over to two children playing in the bay window. "Eva, this is Peter. He's four and a half. And Bella was six last month."

Peter hid behind his mother, while Bella came boldly up to me. "Do you like paddling?" she demanded.

"Very much."

"Goody."

Peter soon got over his shyness, and so did I. Every morning when I came into the dining room, he and Bella shouted, "Eva, Eva," and I hurried to join them, embarrassed and pleased by the attention. Mrs. Nicholson would pour me a cup of coffee. I grew to like the bitter woody taste, and we would discuss plans for the day. In fine weather my task was easy. I took the children to the beach, where we built immense fortresses, paddled, and watched Punch and Judy. If the day was wet, however, it was hard to keep them entertained without disturbing the other guests. One rainy afternoon, at my wits' end, I remembered how, as a little girl, David had sometimes taken me to the forge. I got the hotel taxi to drive us there.

Ian Hunter was at the anvil, hammering a metal bar; he had been apprenticed to his father for nearly two years. For a minute he pounded away. Then he caught sight of me standing in the doorway, a child in either hand. "Hello, Eva. You've been busy."

As I introduced Peter and Bella, his meaning came to me. I

blushed but the children were already pulling towards the furnace. Ian showed them his tools and allowed Bella to have a go with the hammer and Peter to work the bellows. "Is it very hot?" Bella asked.

"Hotter than Hades," Ian said, turning to smile at me.

In the glow of the coals, I saw the faint scar across his eyebrow where he had cut it fighting at Miss MacGregor's. Since then Ian's reputation for troublemaking had steadily deepened; nonetheless I found myself smiling back.

Five years later I was bending over a navigator, syringing the black silk stitches in his palate, when I saw a similar scar. "Norm," I asked, "where did you get this?"

He reached for his pencil and pad. *Scrapping in the schoolyard,* he wrote. *Amazing you noticed, nurse.*

Ian had been dead for eighteen months, but for a moment I felt the heat of the furnace on my face, the chill wind at my back. "Keep still," I said, and refilled the syringe.

On the last day of the month, after I handed over the children, Mrs. Nicholson asked me to join her for supper. I bicycled home at top speed and ran into the house with such a clatter that Lily demanded what was wrong.

"Nothing," I said. "Mrs. Nicholson invited me for dinner. I can't decide what to wear. Perhaps my white dress and the shoes I got for Isobel's party? Maybe I could borrow your jacket?"

"But I'm making toad-in-the-hole." She indicated the bowl of eggs she was beating.

I took in the set of Lily's shoulders, the angry clack of the whisk.

"I'm sorry," I said, more carefully. "She only asked me now. Can't you save some for tomorrow?"

"It's not as good the second day. Besides, your white dress is dirty."

"I'll wear the green one. She knows I don't have grand clothes." I walked around the table. In my mind Lily still towered over me, and I was always surprised to discover this was no longer the case. "Do you want me to finish that?" I asked, pointing at the eggs. Lily shook her head.

I retreated upstairs and fussed over my appearance until the sound of the wireless told me David was safely home. "You look pretty," he said when I stepped into the kitchen. "Where are you off to?"

I explained, trying not to glance in Lily's direction. Clearly she had not mentioned my dinner, but David gave no sign of noticing the omission. "Lucky you," he said. "I've heard the food is excellent. You'll have to tell us all about it."

"'Bye," said Lily from beside the stove.

As I walked down the lane, I fretted over her mysterious disapproval. Why should a dinner invitation make her cross? Looking back, I realised that almost every time she spoke of Mrs. Nicholson, it was to say something critical. She should not have come to Troon without her husband; her ideas about child-rearing were very odd. But the instant I stepped into the hotel dining room such thoughts vanished. Beneath the twinkling chandeliers sat women bright as birds of paradise accompanied by men in dinner jackets. I might have remained gazing at the spectacle indefinitely, if the maître d' had not appeared. He led me across the room and, in one swift movement, had me seated opposite Mrs. Nicholson, glamourous in a deep red dress. She smiled and said she'd ordered me a sherry. "I hope that suits you?"

I would have agreed to anything, drunk any potion, eaten any concoction. The waiter brought menus. The words were like a poem: sautéed, flambéed, seasoned. Mrs. Nicholson made recommendations, and soon we each had a plate of buttered prawns. She asked what I planned to do next. "Insofar as one can have plans these days," she added, spearing a prawn.

It was a question I had no practise in answering. Everyone assumed I would go on living at Ballintyre until, in some vague way, I got married. And my own thoughts were equally vague, daydreams of following Amy Johnson into the air or discovering the source of some great river. I was still pondering my reply as Mrs. Nicholson described her brief career as a research assistant at the university. "I felt like Sherlock Holmes," she said, "tracking down obscure books."

The waiter cleared our plates and set bowls of asparagus soup before us. A second waiter filled our glasses with wine, the same watery gold as the cairngorm brooch I had given Lily for Christmas. "Here's to your future." Mrs. Nicholson raised her glass. "Whatever it may be."

Emboldened by the sherry and the wine, I asked the nature of the illness from which she was recovering.

"I had a miscarriage."

I was so startled I almost dropped my spoon. Of course such events were sometimes hinted at around town, but never, never spoken aloud.

"I was terribly upset," she went on, "but they do say these things happen for a reason, nature's way of taking care of problems. This soup is delicious. Did I ever tell you about our cook's attempt at haggis?"

We were nearly at the end of the meal, eating our chocolate mousse in tiny bites, when she surprised me again. "I must say," she said, "your aunt is a bit of a battle-axe."

"My aunt?"

"She absolutely tyrannises the church choir." Mrs. Nicholson pulled back her shoulders. "'Aren't we being a little too jolly during this hymn?'"

I laughed, as much at my mistake in thinking she meant Lily as at her imitation of Violet.

In the hotel lounge she embraced me, and my eyes filled with tears. But outside I cheered up immediately. I set off down the main street, gliding across the cobblestones, past the Co-op and the butcher's. Near the post office I almost tripped over Tiger, the post-mistress's cat. As I straightened, someone took my arm.

Once more tears threatened. This had been the most wonderful evening of my life, and now here was the girl to remind me of certain inescapable facts: that I was five foot six, that I had a birthmark the size of a shilling on my left thigh, that I was what Lily called cack-handed, that I could not carry a tune, that I had secret companions. Each cobblestone was wholly separate and distinct.

"Do you know what's the matter with you?" she asked, giving me a little shake. "You're drunk."

I stepped beside her docilely. I had read descriptions of men being drunk, but I had never imagined it could be such a pleasant, airy sensation. At the bottom of the lane she stopped. "Don't let them smell your breath," she cautioned, and headed back towards town.

In the kitchen Lily and David were playing cribbage; there was dance music on the wireless, just like they'd been playing at the hotel. "Eva," said David, "did you have a good time?"

I gave a quick account of my evening. "Very la-di-da," said Lily. "Well, madam, it's long past your bedtime."

At first I was happy to return to my usual activities. I played tennis with Isobel, went fishing with David, helped Lily bottle the last of the summer's fruit. As week followed week, however, each day began to seem like a huge, empty loch which it was my duty to fill with a thimble. I remembered Mrs. Nicholson's question and tried to talk to Lily about my future.

"You have a job," she said, "helping with the house. I'm not as young as I used to be, and it's more than I can cope with."

If this had been true, perhaps I would have been content, but for the most part Lily still delegated to me the tasks that were mine at six or seven: laying the table, feeding the hens. The evenings were drawing in, and I felt increasingly confined. After supper the three of us sat in the kitchen. David read or did embroidery. Although his fingers were growing stiff, he still made several fire screens a year for the church fete. Lily mended. I read book after book from the library. Sometimes out of the corner of my eye I saw a chair twitch or a curtain flutter, but when I raised my head everything was motionless, and there was Lily eager to converse.

One evening I came into my chilly room to find the woman sitting on the bed, her raincoat in her lap. "Eva," she said, "you ought to have a job."

"I tried. I spoke to Aunt Lily, but she needs me here."

The woman shook her head. By this time, I could see that she was not really so old. Beneath her brilliant hair, her face was smooth, with only the faintest lines around her deep-set eyes. "Listen," she said. "Lily would give her life for you, with no more fuss than if you asked to borrow a pair of gloves. Meanwhile"—she fiddled with a button of her coat—"she'll take *your* life. Tell David what you want."

That Sunday, I remember, was the harvest festival. On Saturday, David and I carried our offerings to Saint Cuthbert's: two loaves of Lily's bread and a basket of apples. All the way to church I had been trying out different phrases in my head. As we approached the altar, I burst out with my request.

"A job?" David was placing the apples next to a sheaf of corn. "That's not a bad idea. Maybe something in an office. Look at Mr. Cameron's beautiful carrots."

We left the church and walked past the copper beech tree. The leaves were nearly all fallen. As I tidied the grave, David recounted a dream he'd had, something about the Hanscombes, but I was too excited to listen. I was picturing myself in a suit, taking dictation, perhaps even speaking on the telephone.

When he was satisfied, he nodded farewell. "She was a lovely woman, Mrs. Hanscombe," he said at the gate. "I would never have married Barbara without her help."

"How do you mean?" I said, paying attention at last. "You fell in love at the optician's."

"I did, but Barbara took a little longer. Mrs. Hanscombe gave us a chance to get acquainted by asking us to tea every Sunday. Speaking of tea, wasn't there something Lily wanted?"

We halted, each struggling to recall Lily's request. Then I remembered: a packet of digestive biscuits.

We were both quiet on the walk to the Co-op. Perhaps David was preoccupied with his dream. As for me, I was glimpsing that the stories I'd been hearing all my life had been changed in the telling, made into fairy tales for a little girl. Now I have some understanding of why one might want to protect a child, but at the time it gave me an unsettled feeling. Were the facts I had taken for granted going to start shifting like the furniture? Yes, of course—the whole world was shifting—and that unsettled feeling lasted, on and off, for years, until I saw an olive-complexioned man exclaim over an operation and waltz a sister around the ward.

A few days later, at supper, David announced that he had arranged for me to train as a secretary with Mr. Laing, one of the two solicitors in town. "Lily will be able to give you lots of advice," he said when I finished embracing him. "She was a first-rate secretary before she came to take care of us."

Suddenly nervous, I looked across the table at Lily. "What will the hours be?" she asked, pulling her napkin out of its ring.

"Eight-thirty to five, but no Saturdays," David said.

"Well"—she smoothed the napkin over her lap—"I suppose it won't be so different from school."

For the rest of supper she reminisced about her own office experiences: how clients had asked for her specially; how Mr. Bonner, her employer, said she had the fastest fingers in Scotland. The following week we went to Glasgow and I used Mrs. Nicholson's money to buy a skirt, two blouses, and a cardigan; I had never had so many new clothes at one time before.

David had told me Mr. Laing was a nice man and at my brief interview this seemed to be true, but I soon discovered that he seldom emerged from his inner room, the entrance to which was guarded by Miss Nora Blythe. Miss Blythe had run the office for twenty years and looked as if she had spent most of that time squeezed between two ledgers. Immensely upright and efficient, she bullied me to within a blink of tears. I turned out to have the slowest fingers in Scotland. Only Angus, the messenger boy, saved me from misery.

I had been at the office for three weeks when one morning the door swung open and Mr. Wright appeared in his farm clothes. He strode across the room, leaving a tang of manure in his wake, and, before Miss Blythe could prevent him, disappeared into the inner office. "Mr. Laing, this is an outrage." Further remarks were obliterated by the hailstorm of Miss Blythe's typing. Slowly I tapped: "As stated in my letter of the 12th inst."

Half an hour later, when Mr. Laing showed Mr. Wright out, whisky mingled with the manure. "Happy to be of service," Mr. Laing said, and, in a very different tone, "A word, Miss Blythe."

When she emerged, I tried to keep typing, until I heard the unmistakable summons.

"Do you recognise this?" She held out a sheet of paper.

It was the letter I had typed to Mr. Creighton the previous week about the dispute he and Mr. Wright were having over a field by the river.

"You sent this to Mr. Wright, and presumably his letter went to Mr. Creighton."

Beneath Miss Blythe's sardonic gaze, my cheeks glowed. "I'm sorry," I said at last. "I don't know how I could have."

"I imagine you were chattering to Angus. This may cost the firm hundreds of pounds."

"I'm sorry," I repeated. "I'll talk to Mr. Wright on my way home. I'm sure he'll understand."

"You'll do no such thing. You've already caused enough trouble. Just be more careful."

That evening I met the girl loitering outside the forge. "I hear you're in hot water," she said. She was sucking a piece of grass between her teeth.

I remembered her shoving me into a ditch, throwing the stone at Catherine. "You didn't have anything to do with the muddled letters, did you?"

"Of course not, silly." She spat out the grass and disappeared behind the hedge.

In spite of my best efforts, mishaps continued—papers I had filed could not be found, a client was billed for the wrong amount. Once or twice I set traps, made a note of where a document was filed or showed a letter to Angus; naturally nothing happened. As I cycled to and from the office, I argued with the companions in my head. Why would they first help me to get a job and then ruin it? It made no sense. But why should they make sense? Joan's voices, too, had finally betrayed her.

On the last Friday of the month, Mr. Laing called me into his inner sanctum to announce he would have to let me go. Outside, Miss Blythe was waiting. "I'm sorry, Eva. I've always said I could train anyone, but you're just not suited to office life."

Not until I was pedalling home did I take in what had happened: I had been fired. At the bottom of the lane I jumped off my bike. "How could you?" I demanded of the dry grass, the sagging fence, the potholes, the leafless trees.

But the air remained empty. They would not appear to answer my charges. This was their prerogative, to come and go in my life as they pleased, meddling or helping, while I was left to cope with the consequences. I wheeled my bicycle the rest of the way to Ballintyre.

6

Working in the operating theatre was part of every nurse's training and I had duly put in my time there before I met Samuel, but I never did grow comfortable with this aspect of nursing; my job was to tend the body and I hated to watch someone take a knife to the flesh I had bathed and bandaged and fed. Samuel's feelings, however, were the exact opposite. Ordinary doctoring struck him as vague, almost mystical. The patient has a pain; the doctor makes an informed guess and prescribes medicine which may or may not help. But in surgery you could see the problem—a tumour, a broken bone, a malfunctioning joint or organ—and, hopefully, you could fix it.

"I'm like doubting Thomas," he said. "I want to touch the wounds. I know it's a limitation, Eva. When I was training I met certain doctors, nurses too, who had a real gift for diagnosis. But my gift is in my hands; I'm more of an engineer than a doctor."

He underestimated himself—he was unusually generous in talking to his patients—still, when I saw him at work at the operating table, making jokes, pausing to figure out the next cut, deciding just which piece of skin or bone to graft, I recognised that he was in his element. And that no amount of skillful nursing could give a man a new jaw or remove the keloid scars which paralysed his hands.

When I broke the news about Mr. Laing, David laughed and said, Never mind, we can't all be good at office work. Lily was the one who took umbrage. How could they treat me like that? They were meant to be training me. The next day, though, she remarked how glad she was to have my help again. I nodded grimly. I won't be here for long, I wanted to say, but I had no idea what to do next. Working in a shop was out of the question, and no one I knew in Troon needed a nanny.

A week after my dismissal, a letter came from Shona Pyper. In September she and Flo, still inseparable, had gone to Edinburgh to study nursing.

> We have all kinds of high jinks in the hostel. The other girls are grand. Mind you, it's not all fun and games. The sisters are terribly strict, and there are classes from eight until one every day.

Looking at Shona's neat handwriting, I remembered those long afternoons at Miss MacGregor's, making As and Bs and Cs. And now here she was fifty miles away, living the life of Riley.

"What does Shona have to say for herself?" Lily was checking the cupboards, making the shopping list.

I told her. "It sounds smashing."

Lily squinted into the flour bin. "If I were Mrs. Pyper, I wouldn't let a girl Shona's age go off to Edinburgh alone."

"She's not alone. She's with Flo, in a hostel."

"A hostel. She's what—eighteen, nineteen?"

"You went to Glasgow, and you had your own rooms."

"I was thirty-one. Besides, there was a war on."

Watching her purse her lips and add another item to the list, I realised that as far as Lily was concerned we could all three go on living at Ballintyre happily ever after. When she announced she was ready to leave, I said I would stay home. "Are you feeling poorly?" she asked solicitously, code for my monthly visitor.

"No, I'm fine. There's just no need for the two of us when you're not doing a big shop." I seized the newspaper from the table, as if reading it were suddenly a matter of urgency.

"Oh, well, Miss Contrary, keep an eye on the fire."

A few months later my new friend, Daphne, and I would laugh over my tiny rebellion, but at the time I could hardly contain myself. I paced, I put away the breakfast dishes, I filled the coal scuttle. I owe Lily everything, I thought, yet I cannot bear to live this way. When I heard her steps on the path I rushed to the door. "Let me take those," I said, reaching for the groceries.

Usually after a trip into town Lily was full of gossip; today she put away the baking powder and sugar without a word.

"Sit down," I said. "I'll clean the tatties. Have some tea."

Lily sat. She sipped her tea. Silence hung between us like a wet sheet.

"Who did you see in town?" I asked at last.

"I was at the post office." She studied the ivy pattern on her saucer. "Mrs. Hogg told me she'd seen you at the forge."

"Yes, I stopped to say hello to Ian on my way back from the library." The postmistress's arrival to pick up a poker had reminded me I was late for lunch, and I had hurried away. Perhaps she'd thought me rude?

I started to explain but Lily interrupted. "Mrs. Hogg's neither here nor there. The point is, Eva, you're nearly nineteen, too old to run around like a little girl. I asked for a dozen stamps, and Mrs. Hogg said she'd heard Ian had good prospects. In front of the whole queue. I nearly died."

In an instant I understood. "I can't stop talking to my friends because of some old busybody. Ian and I were—"

Lily raised a hand. "I know there's nothing in it, but you're not to go to the forge. Do you hear?"

I bit my lip and nodded.

In bed that night I thought about people linking my name with Ian's. The idea plunged me into a tumult, of pleasure or distress I couldn't tell. The previous week I had run into my first deskmate, Jessie, at the Co-op. Married, with two children already, she asked if I had a beau. I shook my head. "Och, you will soon enough," said Jessie, looking me up and down. "You've turned out bonnier than I expected. What a scrawny wee thing you were at Miss Mac-Gregor's."

Now I gazed at the ceiling, wondering if Jessie was right. David would occasionally remark that I was the image of Barbara, but I had no sense of likeness to the misty woman in the picture over my bed. When I looked in the mirror, I saw only my own face: the dark eyebrows, the straight nose. My hair was the plain brown of beech mast, although Samuel claimed the colour was the same as that of

Mary, Queen of Scots. As for Lily, she sometimes praised my teeth. "Thank goodness they came in straight," she would say. But who besides Lily cared about teeth?

For the rest of the week it rained solidly. On Saturday when I woke to find the sky clear, staying indoors seemed impossible. As soon as breakfast was over I set out for the river. I had intended to take my usual path through the woods. Instead, I crossed the humpbacked bridge and turned down into the fields. Since Lily's scolding I had been gloomy but now, watching the orange-legged oystercatchers peck the sodden grass, my mood lightened. Then I saw a figure coming towards me with such steady purpose it was as if we had an assignation.

"Eva," Ian called. Within a minute we were face-to-face. "It's a grand day."

He was freshly shaven and his eyes, often bloodshot from the furnace, were clear. We began to walk downstream in the direction of my willow tree. Ian talked about his brother Ted, newly enlisted in the Black Watch. "I told him he's daft, but he says we'll all be there soon enough so why not get a head start?"

He could have discussed carburettors or cauliflowers, and I would have been content. Opposite the tree was a gravel spit. Ian picked up a stone and skipped it over the water. It bounced four times. My own effort sank immediately. "I'm hopeless at throwing," I said.

"You just don't know how." He found a flat stone and demonstrated. Then he handed it to me and guided my wrist through the movements. My first throw was no better; the next bounced twice. "There," said Ian. "All you needed was a lesson." We walked on.

I arrived home, flushed and breathless, glad to find David already back from his office. As Lily ladled out the scotch broth, he asked whether she'd gone into town that morning.

"No, I took Mrs. Fisher some soup. Her lumbago's so bad with all the rain she can't even tie her shoes, poor thing."

Mrs. Fisher lived in a cottage across the river. To visit her Lily had followed in my footsteps—from the bridge the gravel spit was in full view. I stared down at the barley floating in my broth, waiting for reproaches, but when she spoke again it was only to ask for the salt. After lunch I did the dishes as quickly as possible and escaped to visit Isobel; we had arranged to hem our winter skirts that afternoon. On the doorstep, however, she greeted me with a change of plan. It was criminal to stay indoors on such a day. How about a round of golf?

She played first, blowing back her fringe and swinging her club hard.

"Good shot," I said.

"No." She grimaced. "It's going in the bunker." Then she turned to me, eyes gleaming. "Can you keep a secret?"

"Of course."

"Gordon and I are engaged."

"Gordon?" I echoed. "Engaged?"

From beneath her blouse she produced a length of wool holding a ring. I praised the small circle of amethysts and asked why it was a secret. Everything about her announcement struck me as romantic except the object. I had met Gordon when Isobel's brother brought him home from university and had not warmed to his damp handshake or his Latin jokes.

"You know Dad," she said. "He'd blow a gasket if I told him I was marrying a student." Being Isobel, though, she was undaunted. She had found an advertisment in the *Ladies' Home Journal* for a nanny in Edinburgh. Last Thursday she had gone for an interview and been hired on the spot. "I'm not mad about children, but these two seemed okay."

"You mean you're leaving?"

"In a fortnight. Why don't you come? There are plenty of jobs, and you even have experience."

Why didn't I? Isobel made it sound so simple. Briefly I pictured a life filled with new people, independence, fun. "Aunt Lily," I muttered, and bent to set my ball on the tee. Isobel strolled off down the fairway. I gripped my club, made a couple of practise swings. Soon I would be all alone, living with David and Lily until I was an old maid, older than Barbara, older than the woman, older than—

"Come on," Isobel called. "After all the shilly-shallying, this had better be a hole in one."

But even as I railed the tide had turned. On Sunday, after church, Lily and David sat me down and asked whether I might want to consider nursing, like Shona and Flo. By next weekend I had filled out an application for Glasgow Infirmary.

"So what made them change their tune?" asked Isobel.

"I think Lily saw me with Ian Hunter."

"Ian," whooped Isobel. "You sly minx."

I could not tell her my real guess, that the companions had engineered the whole thing: Shona's letter, my meeting with Ian, Lily's witnessing thereof. Although I was delighted at the results, their intervention troubled me. After Mr. Laing's, I no longer trusted them. Then one afternoon when Lily and I were sewing name tags on my probationer's uniform and she was talking about the botanical gardens in Glasgow, it suddenly came to me: At long last, I would be rid of the companions. There I would be, smelling the beautiful flowers, going to the cinema, and they would be stuck here, moping around as usual.

"And the orchid house," said Lily. "You feel like you're in Spain."

"Grand," I exclaimed, plying my needle so exuberantly that Lily had to remind me I was not making a fishing net.

After the initial hullabaloo died down, I found ways to keep meeting with Ian but I did not mention Glasgow to him. When I passed the forge, he would often walk a few hundred yards with me. He even attended Saint Cuthbert's and, three pews behind us, belted out the hymns. At the end of the service he came over to say how do you do. David asked whether he'd shoed Mr. Wright's horses this year; Lily asked after his mother. As for me, later Ian claimed I was red as a pillar box.

By early December I was bold enough to agree to a rendezvous by the river. Dusk was falling as I cycled to the bridge, and I could barely make out Ian waiting at the same spot where, years before, Barbara had glimpsed Agnes, the dairymaid who drowned. "Shall we go for a wee stroll?" he said, taking my arm.

At the river's edge he spread a blanket on the grass. We sat down side by side. "Look," I said, "the evening star."

"Venus." He put his arms around me. "Come on. Give me a kiss."

At first Ian's kisses were not so different from those I had been giving and receiving all my life. Then, as he pressed closer, I felt a strange tingling. "No," I said, even as my arms tightened around him.

"Sweetheart," he murmured.

I closed my eyes in a drift of pleasure. When I opened them, a face was watching us over his shoulder. The gypsies, I thought. I pushed Ian away and jumped to my feet. Out of the reeds rose the girl. Her mouth opened, soundlessly, before she turned and ran into the darkness.

"Eva," said Ian, "I'm sorry. Sit down. I'll be good."

As he described the Indian motorcycle his mother was helping him buy for Christmas, I gradually recovered my composure, and by the time we parted my fears were focused on Lily. I told her I'd been at the library all afternoon and, when she believed me, felt so wretched that I vowed to give Ian up. A few days later I was once again making excuses to pass the forge.

At last, on Christmas Eve, I confessed about the infirmary. "Jesus," he said, his face crumpling, "I'll never see you again."

"Of course you will. Glasgow isn't far, and I'll be home for weekends and holidays."

"It won't be the same. You'll be full of fancy city ways. You won't want to be bothered with me."

I argued, even though I guessed he spoke the truth.

We met on New Year's Day at the willow tree to say goodbye. Both our eyes were watery, and as I leaned against him I thought Lily had been right to worry. I could easily have been one of those girls, like Jessie, who married in early haste.

Part II

GLASGOW

7

I left Ballintyre the Monday after New Year's, wearing a navy-blue coat David had given me for Christmas and carrying the suitcase Lily had taken to Glasgow in 1915; it contained my two sets of uniform and my clothes. The nurses' hostel had sent a list, even including the underwear, which Lily insisted on following. I had sneaked in only a couple of items: my favourite green blouse and a pair of shoes. The taxi came on the stroke of eleven and the three of us rode to the station. While David bought my ticket, the first single to Glasgow I had ever purchased, Lily rattled off advice: Don't talk to strangers. Ask a policeman if you need help. Don't skip meals. Always carry a clean handkerchief.

I was relieved when the train wheezed into the station, but as I leaned out of the window to wave goodbye two strangers appeared before me. In place of my beloved ageless father and my aggravating aunt stood an elderly man, stiffer and stouter by the month, and a leaf-thin woman whom the merest breeze could blow away. My girlhood was gone, and its passing had brought David and Lily to the far side of middle age. How had I failed to notice?

But I was eighteen, and the train soon rocked away my sadness. At Glasgow Central when the taxi driver suggested a wee tour of the town, the knowledge that this was just what Lily had warned against added a special piquancy to our trip down Buchanan Street. I stared longingly at the lighted shops and bustling pavements. Soon I would be among this glamourous crowd. The nurses' hostel bore a strong resemblance to the grammar school in Troon, and as I stepped inside the same combination of floor wax, disinfectant, and cabbage smells greeted me. I gave my name, and the porter said, "Good afternoon, Nurse McEwen. Nasty weather."

I was still marvelling at my title as he led me upstairs to my room and pointed out the rules on the back of the door. "The bathroom is down the hall. Supper is at six-thirty."

The room was small and spartan: a single bed, a chest of drawers, a desk and chair, a wardrobe, an easy chair. The walls were a greenish grey, the curtains a greyish green. The sole decoration was a calendar. That this was to be my new home seemed impossible. I opened the suitcase and began to unpack, but after only a couple of skirts, I faltered. The sight of the neatly folded clothes which Lily had ironed and packed the day before made me sink down on the edge of the bed. In my entire life I had not spent a single night away from Ballintyre. Of course David and Lily would write and I would go back for holidays, but never again would I have the certainty of being in their company day after day.

I might have spent the rest of the evening sitting beside my half-empty suitcase, save for a knock at the door. "Come in," I called, standing to meet a stranger.

A dark, curly-haired girl peered round the door in comical fashion and introduced herself. Daphne lived next door and had come to take me to supper. As she led the way downstairs, she told me that the previous occupant of my room had quit just before Christmas. "Some sort of breakdown. Poor girl."

I nodded, my attention fixed on the hem of her uniform, considerably shorter than my own. Mine had been measured by Lily to be exactly the regulation three inches below the knee. In the dining room, amid the din of cutlery and conversation, I asked questions and listened to Daphne's advice. "Avoid Sister McTavish. She'll have your guts for garters. Graham is a good egg. Volunteer for the dispensary. It's painless and gets you a gold star."

Back in my room, as I laid my clothes in the chest of drawers, I recalled Daphne jumping up to fetch me another cup of tea. How much easier it was to embark on a friendship without having to look over my shoulder.

The next day I found myself plunged into ceaseless work. In my daydreams I had imagined myself taking the pulse of pale men, holding my cool hand to the foreheads of feverish children, but mostly I had been preoccupied with living in Glasgow. I had paid little attention to the fact that student nurses worked sixty hours a week and had to study as well. When was there time for Shona's high jinks?

Within a few weeks I felt much as I had at Mr. Laing's. I did not seem able to do anything right, either during lectures or on the wards, and it was small consolation to know that this time the errors were my own. My first day on the ward, Sister caught me accepting a peppermint from a patient, and it was downhill from there. I could not keep all the do's and don'ts straight. I understood there was a correct way to give an injection or treat a disease; why did it matter, though, how I rolled a bandage or made a bed? Worse than all this, I was afraid of pain, of wounds. I closed my eyes even when injecting the dummy.

Daphne, who was three months ahead of me, insisted that the work got easier, that everyone made mistakes, but that did not seem to be true of my classmates. In the few minutes each night before I fell asleep, I racked my brain for alternatives. Might I be qualified to work in a library like Mrs. Nicholson? Or perhaps there was something I could do in a hotel? I was seriously contemplating giving notice when, after several days of shivering and coughing, I fainted during anatomy. The sister had paused in listing the bones of the wrist to reprimand my cardigan; even on the coldest days, nurses were forbidden to wear anything over their short-sleeved uniforms. As I reached to remove the garment, I slid to the floor.

I came round in the women's ward of the infirmary. The nurse who held a glass of water to my lips told me I had bronchitis. "Don't go," I begged as she made to leave.

"Quiet, dear," she said, and whisked away.

She was busy, not unkind, but later when patients made the same appeal to me, I would remember the searing loneliness of those hours, my bed like an island of one, and try to find an extra minute to stay and talk to them. Meanwhile, when Lily came to visit, only pride prevented me from begging her to take me home; I scarcely heard the strange story she told of how, only a few months old, I had escaped my crib and nearly fallen down the stairs.

As my strength returned, day by day, I drifted closer to shore. Watching the nurses, I could see that the apparently petty rules made sense: knowing how to do the simple things—plump a pillow, take a pulse—made it possible to do the complicated ones—stop a haemorrhage, save a life. By the time I recovered, I had missed so many weeks I had to start the training over again, but everything was different; now I actually wanted to be a nurse.

Any lingering doubts were swept away by the prospect of war. Almost from one day to the next, the hazy rumours from Europe clarified into dark ferocious facts; Chamberlain's umbrella became a joke. Blackout blinds were hung in the infirmary and the hostel. Gas masks and ration books were issued. Signs pointed the way to air raid shelters. David wrote that he was trying to get into the Home Guard. Ian enlisted in the Royal Scots, and Isobel joined the WRAC. Like the other probationers, I complained bitterly about not being qualified in time.

In January 1940, the air raids started. Night after night we woke to the sound of the sirens, and at the infirmary a memo was posted: What to do in the event of an air raid. At the first warning, all patients were to be conducted to the cellars. In practise, however, with only two nurses to a ward, this proved impossible. Less than half the patients had been carried down when the all-clear sounded. The memo was revised. Ambulatory patients should make their own way to the cellar; everyone else was to be placed beneath their beds. Even this proved impractical and more dangerous to some patients than the raids themselves. Finally the night nurses settled for sing-alongs.

At the hostel the drill was simpler. We were to make our way promptly, with our gas masks, to the boiler room, where old benches from the dining hall had been set up. Sometimes we had sing-alongs there too; the sister in charge of probationers turned out to have a surprisingly good voice. Or sometimes Daphne and I played Animal, Vegetable, or Mineral. But that sort of fun only happened when the raids began early. Usually the heat of the boiler room and the dim light—reading or sewing were impossible, though some nurses knitted—lulled us into a stupour from which the all-clear roused us. On the worst nights we were barely back in bed before the sirens started again.

We grew pale and short-tempered. The nurses who were on night duty became objects of envy; at least they could rest, undisturbed, during the day. But when my turn came, it was harder than I expected, even with blackout blinds, to fall asleep. I lay in bed, listening to the maid sweeping the corridor, and thought of Ballintyre and the birds singing in the apple tree outside my window. At last I nodded off to dreams filled with missed trains and lost objects. I arrived on duty at 9 P.M., heavy-headed, and was sent to men's surgical. "Just my luck," muttered the staff nurse, on hearing that this was my first night. The two of us had twenty-seven men in our care.

Her strong Glasgow accent was not unlike Daphne's but she herself showed no trace of Daphne's kindness and humour. During the next few hours, as she chivvied me from task to task, her forehead never once unfurrowed, even when a drunk brought in at closing time with a broken ankle burst into a lusty version of "Donald, where's y'er troosers?" Finally at one o'clock, with everything more or less under control, she announced she was going to dinner.

"Watch the drip on number eleven," she said, handing me the keys to the dangerous drugs cupboard. "Bed number four is in trouble."

She marched away and in the wake of her departure one of those odd silences fell when, for a few minutes, no one was snoring or groaning or crying out, and from behind the drawn screens of number four, which I had passed a hundred times that evening, I heard tiny mouselike gasps. In all my thoughts of nursing, strange to say, it had never once occurred to me that some patients failed to recover. Even performing last offices on the pink-and-white dummy we used for bandages and injections had failed to prepare me.

Now I stood beside the flimsy screens, listening intently, until some mixture of pride and compassion forced me inside. In the glow of the night-light a slender man lay propped on several pillows, head lolling, eyes closed. I was struck by the ordinariness of his striped pyjamas, similar to David's, and then by how youthful his face was in spite of grey hair. (Later I encountered other patients in whom pain had lessened, not deepened, the marks of age.) As he stammered from one breath to the next, I clasped my hands and counted like I used to do between the flash of lightning and the peal of thunder, as if the interval would reveal some crucial distance. I was reaching hesitantly for his pulse, a wholly useless gesture I was terrified to make, when from a nearby bed a voice whispered, "Bedpan, nurse."

By the time I returned, he was gone. I don't know for how long I remained, counting into the hundreds, hoping for one more gasp, before I heard the staff nurse's footsteps.

"He died," I told her. "Number four. I couldn't stop him."

At my babble, her frown intensified. She held out her hand, not in comfort but for the keys. "Pull yourself together, Nurse McEwen. Off you go to dinner, and pick up a shroud on your way back."

A shroud, I thought. Where on earth would I find that in the middle of the night? But when I asked, the porter took me to a room lined floor to ceiling with neatly folded garments. "Adult?" he demanded. "Small, medium, or large?"

And suddenly I understood that the other great business of the infirmary, besides helping the sick to return to the world, was helping them to leave it. Yet how seldom anyone spoke of this. Only Father Wishart and Samuel acknowledged our role as watchers at that perilous threshold. Samuel told me that the first time a patient died on the operating table, he had sliced into the chest cavity and begun to massage the heart by hand, shouting for the man to come back. "I couldn't believe there was nothing to be done," he said. "The anaesthetist had to pull me away."

Walking back to the ward, carrying the flimsy shroud through the darkened corridors, I thought of Barbara. I was glad she had died at home with people who knew her name, who were not afraid to take her hand.

I could not write of this to David or Lily, but some of it made its way into my letters to Ian. He turned out to be a surprisingly eloquent correspondent, who outwitted the censors to let me know he was in Algeria. I was glad to hear from him, both for his news and for the kudos of having a friend on active service. I wrote back promptly—after all he was fighting for king and country—but when Daphne invited me to join her and Arthur and Arthur's mate, Roy, for an evening, I accepted without a qualm. Over fish and chips, she and I took turns telling stories about the infirmary; by this time I had learned from her how to transform even my worst adventures into comic episodes. The men shook their heads and blinked with laughter. Then we made our way to the Odeon.

Although Roy and I went out on three or four occasions, I can barely recall his face, perhaps because we were almost always in the darkness, of either the cinema or the blackout. I do remember that first time, walking back to the hostel, when he slipped his arm around my waist and I leaned towards him. Suddenly someone was tugging at my sleeve. I leapt back, but it was only Daphne. "Two minutes till curfew," she whispered.

Between the patients and the nurses, my life in Glasgow was the exact opposite of what it had been at Ballintyre: Every hour was filled with people. It was a rare event when, after an especially arduous day—I had just started as a scrub nurse in the theatre—I found myself walking back to the hostel alone. I was enjoying my brief solitude, pondering whether to stop at the pie shop, when the sirens broke out.

"Bloody nuisance," Daphne always said at such moments, and I had joined in her grumbling as if the raids were indeed a minor irritation. But in the dark street, I was afraid. One of the day's patients had been a casualty of last night's bombing; most of his stomach was missing. The nearest shelter was several streets away. I took refuge in the doorway of a haberdasher's where Daphne and I had tried in vain to buy elastic the week before.

Almost immediately came the crash of an explosion, followed by the barking of air-raid guns and another much louder bang. A scorched, acrid smell filled the air. I reached for my gas mask, but the thought of the clammy rubber against my face was repulsive. Trembling, I began to recite:

> *"Wee, sleekit, cow'rin,' tim'rous beastie,*
> *O, what a panic's in thy breastie!*
> *Thou need na start awa sae hasty,*
> *Wi' bickering brattle!"*

On the word *brattle* a bomb fell. For a few seconds the light and noise blew everything away, including fear. The sounds of glass breaking, beams cracking, masonry falling filled the night.

When at last the noise stopped, I raised my head to discover that the dark sky and darker buildings had disappeared. The doorway was completely blocked. I groped my way forward and tugged at whatever my hand encountered. A brick shifted and rubble tumbled down. No one knew I was here; I would never be found. "Help," I cried. "Help." But it was hard to believe that anything, even sound, could escape this prison.

I was starting on the poem again when from nearby came a scraping sound. "Hello," I called. "Is someone there?"

No answer. The scraping continued. To the fear of being buried alive was added a new fear. In the infirmary, rumours circulated about gangs of men who looted during the raids and, it was whispered, interfered with women.

I was wondering whether to risk crying out again, when something grazed my cheek. I screamed. An eerie silence descended.

At last someone spoke. "Don't be afraid."

Years before, the same voice had said, "What a cosy house." Now the girl started on the poem's second verse.

> *"I'm truly sorry man's dominion,*
> *Has broken nature's social union. . . ."*

Somehow there was an opening in the doorway, just large enough for me to squeeze out. In the street two familiar figures were waiting. The light of the fires glinted off the woman's hair. "Are you all right?" she asked.

I nodded, speechless.

The girl began to dust my cape, slapping vigourously at the fabric. I had not seen her since the night she spied on Ian and me beside the river; even in the darkness, I sensed her glee. As she moved on to my skirt the all-clear sounded. I found my voice and announced I was going back to the hostel.

"We'll walk with you," said the woman.

"There's no need," I said. "Really."

But she stepped forward and took one arm, the girl the other. Even through my uniform their hands seemed colder than I remembered. Without a word we headed down the street. At the corner neighbours were passing pails of water towards a blazing shop. A man at the end of the chain spotted me. Our white caps were unmistakable. "Good night, nurse," he called.

On either side, the companions tightened their grip.

8

I marked off the stages of my training like the stages in high jumping, and almost in spite of myself I grew competent. Soon I knew
what to do in the case of a ruptured ulcer or an asthma attack; I
could change a dressing or give a transfusion or hold the hand of a
dying man. The air raids had dwindled, horses became common in
the city streets, and almost everything was rationed or unavailable.
Penicillin, the new miracle drug, appeared. Back in Troon, David
and Lily were both absorbed in war work. Too old for uniform,
David helped plan manoeuvres for the Home Guard and gave lectures on German strategy. Lily worked at the Station Hotel, now a
convalescents' home, as a bookkeeper and tea lady. On one of my
monthly visits she had me show her how to tie a sling. The beaches
where I had played with the Nicholson children were once more as

Barbara had known them, lined with coils of wire. Only the companions were exempt from the tasks of war.

Since the night of the air raid, I had often met the woman in her old-fashioned clothes, walking down the busy pavements, or the girl loitering outside the hostel. Perhaps I should have been grateful to them, but I soon convinced myself I would have been discovered shortly—the rescue squads were amazingly efficient—and I found their reappearance hard to bear. I had been certain that in coming to Glasgow I was leaving them behind. Now it seemed that all along they had planned to accompany me.

The one saving grace was that they never visited the infirmary. Nonetheless, I worried Daphne might notice the change in me, but, like Isobel, she remained oblivious. What she did notice was my lack of a beau. Arthur and Roy had moved on but the wards were thronged with military personnel, both patients and doctors, and Daphne flitted happily from one romance to the next. After an evening out she would come to my room, cheeks flushed, clothes awry, for cocoa. "Och, we had a grand time," she would say. When she reproached me for being standoffish, I argued that people were always being transferred. All the more fun, she said.

How could I tell her that I longed to follow her example but, after my evening with Bernard, feared disaster. A senior medical student, Bernard had been assigned to the women's ward soon after I moved there. Tall, with blue eyes and dark hair, he had grown up in Oban and, at moments of excitement, lapsed endearingly into Gaelic. On the ward we started calling out *"Ceud míle fáilte,"* whenever he appeared. I asked about the Highlands, the setting of so many of David's stories, and he told me about a cave on the shores of Loch Fyne where Bonnie Prince Charlie had waited for a boat to carry him over to France. "He was a brave man," Bernard said, "to hide in a wee dark hole with a price on his head and nothing but hills and heather for miles around." Only later when I saw Glenaird, the valley where Barbara had grown up, did I fully appreciate his descriptions of the lonely landscape.

One evening, when we both finished early, Bernard invited me to the cinema. In the Empire the usher led us unhesitatingly to the third back row. Roy had once slipped her a shilling to get seats there; now it seemed she knew already that Bernard and I were a couple. I felt a little knot of excitement. For the last fortnight I'd been noticing his earnest smile. After a decent interval, halfway through a Pathé news report on land girls, Bernard slid his arm around me. And after another, I put my head on his shoulder. Would he take my hand, I wondered.

Within a few minutes, however, I felt an odd prickling sensation, a scratching between my shoulder blades, not unlike what I sometimes felt on the wards when a patient needed me but was too shy to call. Cautiously I raised my head to glance around. The light of the screen showed me only strangers, rows of men and women, their eyes fastened on the pictures or each other. I turned back to Bernard but the prickling persisted; it was hard even to sit still. For a second time I scanned the audience, and only then did I realise who I was looking for. I could not help pulling away, as if the screen demanded my urgent attention.

Bernard was a nice young man. He pretended to cough and released me. The news finished and we both concentrated on the film, something American, the men with short ties and funny accents. Afterwards, walking back to the hostel, I was very animated, commenting on the picture, asking about Bernard's family. His replies were courteous but brief. "Well, Nurse McEwen," he said, at the gate of the hostel, "this has been a pleasure."

"Bernard," I protested.

From the darkness around us came the muffled sounds of other nurses and their beaux, making the most of the few minutes before curfew. Of course he could not see my expression, but I stared up at Bernard, silent, pleading, until he bent down and, whether by accident or design, planted a kiss on my ear.

In bed that night I berated myself—why let my stupid imagination ruin everything?—and next day on the ward I continued in my emphatic cheerfulness, joking with the patients and the ward maid. A couple of times I caught Bernard eyeing me, but he kept his distance. I was not entirely sorry when a few weeks later he was transferred to Aberdeen.

Other outings followed a similar pattern, and I never knew whether to blame the companions or myself. They did not appear but instead sent themselves into my mind. My sense returned of a hidden deformity which must, at all costs, be concealed; I dreaded that the young men who slid their hands under my coat would somehow discover my shame.

In the midst of these difficulties, my second stint of night duty came as a relief. Daphne claimed the nights were dull, now that the raids had slackened, but I liked the long slow hours. By day the infirmary buzzed with efficiency: birth, life, death—everything kept in its proper place. Whereas under cover of darkness, anything seemed possible. Patients confided in me and I listened, doing my best to offer comfort and conceal amazement. How tangled people's lives were and how many, besides myself, had problems they could hint at only to a stranger.

It was during this time that I had the conversation with Father Wishart about the hospital ghost and what it is that makes the dead walk. I remember on the next occasion when I met the woman, I studied her with special care. It was a rainy afternoon, and I was at the library choosing books for Daphne when she sidled up to suggest a Thomas Hardy novel. I glanced anxiously around—our only witness was an elderly man, drowsing over the paper—and explained that Daphne had asked for Zane Grey.

"Oh, I don't know those. You'll have to tell me about them."

She was as real to me as she had always been. I saw the pulse beating in her temple, the flicker of those deep grey eyes. She did not seem unhappy, but then she did not seem like a ghost either.

In 1942, shortly after I passed the dreaded Preliminary exams, the burns unit opened. Modelled on the famous unit at East Grinstead near London, it made the front page of the newspapers: SCOTLAND CAN TREAT BURNS AT LAST. And the following year, soon after I became a fully qualified nurse, Daphne and I volunteered for duty there; she had heard the work was interesting and the hours better than in the main infirmary. Sister MacKenzie, a diminutive, sweet-faced woman with a reputation for discipline, greeted us. "I'll tell you now," she said, "this kind of nursing isn't for everyone. The patients can be trying, and Dr. Rosenblum"—her eyes seemed to take in every square inch of our aprons—"has very particular standards."

As we approached the ward, the usual mix of disinfectant and cabbage filled the air, but the noise was extraordinary: music, shouts, the clatter of wheels, a sudden bang, more like a soccer match than a hospital.

"Morning, Sister," called a man near the door. "Introduce us to the pretty nurses?" Where his nose should have been were two white stumps.

"Now, Archie, behave yourself."

I kept my eyes fixed on Sister's apron, trying not to see the blurred features and twisted limbs. Some of the men sprouted tubes of flesh from unlikely places: a cheek, a forearm. Later I learned these were the pedicle grafts, known as "dangle 'ums," and paid them no more heed than their owners; at the time, however, it was all I could do not to run from the ward. And on every side voices catcalled, shouted questions and compliments. These were not patients as I knew them. These were restless, insubordinate pilots, soldiers, men.

Back at the entrance, Sister patted my arm and told Daphne to get me a cup of tea before rounds started. In the nurses' room I sat near an open window while Daphne perched on the sill, chatting about what film to take her mother to and the new underwear at Baker's. Ever since my first evening at the infirmary, I had loved watching her talk. All her features were slightly too large and so vivid that on half a dozen occasions I heard her unjustly reprimanded for wearing makeup. On the wards, patients reached towards her, hoping that her robust good health might be contagious.

"Six coupons for a pair of knickers," she exclaimed. "Still, I tried on Lydia's and they were grand."

By the time an orderly came to fetch us, she had jollied me into a semblance of calm. I was able to join the other nurses and medical students around the first bed. From my position at the back the patient was happily hidden, but I had a clear view of the man standing over him. He was as tanned as if he had spent a whole summer on the beach. Glancing around, he caught my eye and gave a quick smile. One of those older medical students who were showing up more and more as the war dragged on, I thought, and let my gaze slide away. Then he said, "Good morning, everyone," and I realised this was Dr. Rosenblum.

"We have two choices," he explained, gesturing towards the patient. "We can continue with the smaller grafts from the thigh, bacon strips, which lower the risk of infection but are often a little patchy. Or we can go for a larger graft, more susceptible to infection but with a better chance of making Phil resemble Valentino." He verified a couple of points with Sister, then, turning back to the bed, said, "Any thoughts, Philip?"

Beside me, I sensed my own astonishment mirrored in Daphne. For a doctor to consult a nurse was unheard of, let alone a patient. Philip's response was inaudible, but Rosenblum was clearly pleased. "Good man," he said, clapping him on the shoulder. "We'll start on Tuesday and do our damnedest."

With the next couple of patients it was just Hello, how's it going? Then we clustered round the bed of another heavily bandaged figure. Brian had crashed his plane last year, the nurse in front of me whispered. Nine days ago they had operated on his wrists to remove scar tissue and apply skin grafts. Today the theatre dressings would be changed and they would see if the grafts had taken. Almost in spite of myself I edged closer. The rowdy patients fell silent. With each layer of acriflavine gauze the staff nurse lifted I could feel the tension rise, until the ward radio—Harry Lauder singing "I'll tak' the high road"—was the only sound. Brian's hands emerged unpromisingly scarlet, curled like chicken's feet.

Dr. Rosenblum bent to examine them, holding each hand in

turn and gently flexing the fingers. "Brian," he announced, "you'll be playing the piano for Christmas." And that was when he seized the sister and, to the last bars of Harry Lauder, waltzed her round the ward.

For the next few days I continued to feel faint whenever I came on duty, but as I got to know the patients I soon learned to overlook their grotesque injuries. Most of them were airmen severely burned about the face and hands. In spite of all official warnings, they persisted in removing their goggles and gloves. "You can't fight the Jerry with gloves on," one pilot told me. Some of them had been in the unit since the beginning, and it was they who taught me how to identify the different kinds of infection that threatened a graft, how to manipulate dressings and syringe oral stitches.

After my days on the ward, I sometimes found myself in the evenings lingering before the mirror. My face, which I had regarded as such an intimate part of me, seemed different now that I understood how provisional the features were. I could lose my nose or chin, have cheeks framed by the pale skin of my buttocks, a jaw built from a rib bone, a mouth that refused to stay in the centre of my face. Standing there, wiggling my eyebrows, stretching my lips, I wondered would I have been one of those women who stood by their damaged men, recognising the beloved person beneath the disfigurement? Or would I have fled? And of course the question was not always so simple, for some men were vastly altered, not just outwardly but inwardly. Our most difficult patient, a famous fighter pilot, treated everyone, from Samuel to the ward maid, with bitter contempt. After he called me a stupid bitch—I forgot the sugar in his tea—Sister had the porters wheel him out of the ward. His bed remained in the corridor for a week before he muttered, "Sorry."

I had been working on the unit for a little over a month when, coming off duty one afternoon, I discovered it had begun to rain. As I hesitated in the doorway, watching the fat drops bounce off the pavement and wishing I had brought an umbrella, the woman joined me. "Wait here," she said. "It'll ease up soon. And straighten your cap." Briskly, in her raincoat, she headed down the drive.

I stared after her, twitching my cap into place. She had never appeared at the infirmary before and I was furious at the breach of one more boundary. She was not even a good weather prophet; with each passing minute the rain grew heavier. At last, further delay seemed pointless and I plunged out. I was nearly at the street when a shout came: "Nurse McEwen!"

Samuel—Dr. Rosenblum, as I still thought of him—was hurrying towards me, waving a black umbrella. He had just come from working on Donald Bullman's ears.

Donald was one of our few civilians, an accountant who'd been trapped in a burning office, trying to save the ledgers. We had had several conversations about homing pigeons, which in peacetime he bred and raced. I asked how the operation had gone, and Dr. Rosenblum held up crossed fingers. "Ears are tricky," he said. "If only men could wear their hair long." Past the pub and the row of shops, he talked about the difficulties of shaping cartilage. Daphne made fun of Samuel's habit of lecturing, but I found it endearing. Most doctors behaved as if we nurses weren't capable of understanding anything more complicated than a tonsillectomy. Crossing the street to the hostel, Samuel checked himself. "Aren't you due a day off soon?" he said.

"This coming Wednesday."

"I'm off then too. Perhaps we could go to the cinema, have supper?"

From the moment I first caught sight of Samuel standing beside Philip's bed, I had watched him, but no more than everyone else did, patients and nurses alike; he was lord of the unit. Both rank and age—I guessed him, wrongly, to be in his late rather than his early thirties—had made him seem beyond daydreams. Now, under the shelter of the umbrella, he turned to me and I did not turn away. I had grown up among blue-eyed people, but gazing into Samuel's brown eyes, I seemed to glimpse something I had been searching for for a long time. "I'm going to visit my family," I said. "Would you like to come?"

In the days that followed, I regretted my invitation twenty times over. When I tried to imagine Ballintyre through Samuel's eyes, everything seemed shabby and old. And of course I worried about Lily's and David's reactions. I wrote saying I was bringing a guest, Dr. Rosenblum, I underlined, both glad and sorry that there was no time for a reply. On Wednesday when I came into the bus station and saw him standing beside the ticket office, I would gladly have fled. But he was already walking towards me, looking surprisingly dapper in a dark hat and navy suit, the waistcoat buttoned snugly over his girth. Ian and Roy—even Bernard—had shared a boyish quality; you could still picture them kicking a football in the playground, but Samuel was a man, solidly planted in his life and his work.

While we waited, he told me that the Russians had entered Romania, and by the time we boarded the bus I was remembering again how much I liked him. Halfway down the aisle he slid into a seat and I followed. A bell sounded. The driver, a young woman not much older than myself and no taller than the unit sister, started up the engine. As we bumped through the suburbs of Glasgow and into the open countryside, Samuel told me about his family. He had grown up in Edinburgh, where his father was a jeweller; his two brothers were both doctors and his sister taught at the university.

"They sound awfully clever," I said.

"That is the one thing everyone agrees on about Jews."

"Are you a Jew?"

He burst out laughing, and I caught the flash of his fillings. "With a name like Samuel Rosenblum?" Then he saw my face. "I'm sorry, Eva. Most people guess."

He began to talk about how his grandfather had come to Edinburgh from Vienna. I nodded, trying to recall what I knew. Disraeli was a Jew, so was Dreyfus. At Sunday school we read stories about the chosen people. Moses had led them to safety across the Red Sea. And they had different customs, like not eating pork. What if Lily served ham for lunch?

At the next village the bus slowed; a number of passengers rose to their feet. Suddenly a voice said, "I wish I had a white feather for you, my lad."

An elderly woman in a threadbare coat shuffled past. It must be she who had spoken, but what on earth did she mean? Then I recalled David's describing the gangs of women who had roamed the streets during the last war, handing out white feathers to young men not in uniform.

I reached the front of the bus just as she was negotiating the first step. "Excuse me," I said. "He's a doctor at the infirmary, a surgeon."

The woman turned and I saw skin the colour of plaster, eyes swimming behind thick spectacles. "What use is a doctor to me? I lost three sons in the Great War." With painful slowness, she clambered down the remaining steps into the village street.

I returned to my seat, cheeks burning, not daring to meet Samuel's gaze. What a fool he must think me. But for the second time since we boarded the bus, he was apologising to me. "I should have warned you," he said. "All of us younger doctors get comments."

I teased the fingers of my gloves and told him about her sons. "It must be as if they died in vain."

"Poor woman," said Samuel. "I don't know about the last war, the casualties were appalling, but I do know that nothing is more important than stopping Hitler." It was exactly what everyone said, but something in his voice made me understand that he meant it quite literally.

For the rest of the journey he asked about my family. I told the familiar stories about Barbara's saving Keith Hanscombe and meeting David at the optician's, her death, and Lily coming to take care of me. Soon we were in Troon, passing the grammar school and Saint Cuthbert's. Lily was waiting outside the Co-op, wearing her best blue felt hat.

She greeted Samuel warmly and he shook her hand and said she mustn't dare call him doctor. As we walked back to Ballintyre he asked about the convalescents' home, and she waxed eloquent on the subject of diet and bandages. At the forge I glimpsed a figure bent over the glowing furnace. Ian, I thought. Then I remembered he had died the previous spring, of dysentery, in North Africa; his mother's hair had turned white overnight.

David was in the garden, planting potatoes. He put aside his spade to welcome Samuel. While I helped Lily with lunch, thankfully no ham in sight, the two of them discussed the Second Front. They shared similar views about American involvement: Pearl Harbor was a tragedy; still, it had got us what we needed.

That evening on the bus back to Glasgow, Samuel said how much he liked Lily and David. Oh, good, I said vaguely. All I could think about was whether he liked me. Then, at last, he put his arm around my shoulders. I glanced anxiously up and down the aisle. The bus was darker than any cinema; the couple in the seat behind us were snoring softly. At first I could not help looking around every few minutes, but as the miles slid by and Samuel held me close and I felt nothing other than his embrace, the intervals between my searching grew longer and longer.

9

A fortnight after our trip to Troon, Samuel took me to his favourite restaurant, the Trattoria. He ordered us spaghetti with sardines. "And a bottle of chianti."

"Chianti?" jeered the waiter. "Not a chance, guv. We've been dry as a Sunday school since last year."

Samuel watched him limp off towards the kitchen with a frown. "I must have fallen from grace," he said. "I had a nice bottle here just a couple of months ago."

"I don't mind. Wine makes me dizzy." I fingered a small ochre stain on the tablecloth. "I didn't mean to offend you the other day, on the bus. I really didn't know you were a Jew."

"Eva, I'm the one who should apologise for being so touchy. The world is full of people who don't like us."

"But you're the most popular doctor at the hospital."

His face changed in a way I hadn't seen before, not the tightening of the lips when he discovered a failed graft nor the widened eyes that greeted good news, but a sharp twist, as if all the muscles under the skin were tugging in different directions. "Up to a point," he said. "Last Christmas I went out to dinner with some friends. I was working late, and I hadn't had a chance to go to the bank. When the bill came I asked Hugh Bailey, the cardiologist, for a loan. 'Oh,' he said, 'the pound of flesh.' Even with people I've known for years, I only have to do the smallest thing and I'm a kike, a Yid, a person they despise."

The waiter placed large bowls before us and filled our water glasses, ostentatiously, to the brim. I found the long thin strands of spaghetti hard to manage, but Samuel seemed to have no trouble twirling them into neat mouthfuls. He told me about celebrating the Sabbath at home, about Passover and Hanukkah. "I was always out of step with the other boys. While everyone else was listening to stories of Robin Hood and Ivanhoe, my mother was reading me Jewish folk tales. My favourite was about a boy who goes hunting for treasure and, after many adventures, meets a wise man instead." He smiled. "Then there was the tale of the dybbuk. You've probably never heard of that. A dybbuk is a spirit who takes possession of a person."

I felt as if my skin had suddenly expanded, as if every nerve in my body were reaching towards him, like that Indian goddess with so many hands, trying to grasp his meaning. I asked Samuel to explain.

"A young woman is possessed by the spirit of a dead man. She looks the same but she acts like him, and when she speaks, his words come out of her mouth. My mother loves charades, and she always read the dybbuk's part in a hoarse, deep voice. After she finished, I would lie in bed terrified. Every sound was a spirit trying to climb in the window."

I remembered the giant of David's stories and how I had had similar imaginings. "What happens?" I asked.

"Eventually the spirit is exorcised, by a rabbi."

"And the girl?" I managed.

"Oh." He gave a small nod. "She dies."

While he organised another mouthful of spaghetti, I stared unseeing at my plate. I had grown so used to dividing myself into the spoken and the unspoken that I seldom considered the alternative. Now the pleasure of sharing my secret shimmered before me. I saw my life become a simple room, the floor polished, the walls white as wood anemones.

Samuel was talking again, about his father. Someone had scrawled FIFTH COLUMNIST across his shop window because he'd written a letter to the newspaper about the *Struma*. "He's been on George Street for thirty years, and suddenly he's a spy and seven hundred Jews are allowed to drown." Samuel's indignant gesture sent a strand of spaghetti flying across the room, but he was too busy to notice. Mr. Rosenblum was on the board of several charities and had personally taught a dozen boys to read. "He's never turned away a soul," Samuel said, "on the basis of creed, class, or money."

Dimly I recalled the *Struma*, the boat filled with Jewish refugees moored for months outside Istanbul, but before I could question him further a bearded man stood over our table, flourishing a bottle of red wine. Samuel had fixed his daughter's cleft palate last spring—his brother-in-law owned the Trattoria—and so our evening ended as a jolly threesome.

During the weeks that followed, Samuel and I fell into a kind of routine. His hours were even longer than my own but usually we managed to go to the cinema on Friday or Saturday and sometimes during the week we would go to Tommy's Café to eat shepherd's pie and chat about our days. On the unit he treated me just as he did everyone else: kindly, straightforwardly. No one would ever guess, Daphne assured me. She herself was in love with a radiologist, a tall, witty man with slightly crossed eyes who seemed to dote on her.

Early in January a pilot named Neal Cunningham was transferred to the unit from Aberdeen. I was off duty the day he arrived, but the following morning, as I made the beds with Mollie, the ward probationer, the men could talk of little else. Patient after patient described how the newcomer had kept them awake with his screams. Bloodcurdling, claimed Archie. Like a wolf, said Brian.

Neal, when at last we reached his bed in the far corner, lay with the covers drawn up to his chin. His face was dark as a Negro's, not from the burns themselves but from the tannic acid they still used as a coagulant at the first-aid stations. His wavy brown hair—he must have worn a helmet—was the only clue to his colouring. "Och, Neal," Mollie said, "I hear you behaved like a football hooligan in the night."

From behind the black mask came a murmured apology. His skin was so badly burned that even to whisper seemed an effort, but that did not dull his nocturnal screams.

The same scenario was repeated the next night, and the next. Sedatives had no effect and soon Neal was moved to one of the private rooms, which—since Samuel's decision that officers and ordinary ranks would share the wards—were usually empty. Almost everyone, from the matron to the maids, had complained about this lack of segregation, but Samuel stood firm. "If you're waiting for a new jaw you don't need solitude," he had insisted. "You need someone to beat you at dominoes and make bad jokes about your dentist."

That evening as I left the unit, I decided to look in on Neal. Something about his helplessness engaged my sympathy. When I stepped into his room, he was sitting up in bed, staring at the door as if Göring himself might appear.

"I just came to say good night," I said, drawing my cloak closer. I was abashed to have caused such fear.

"Thank you, nurse. Good night."

Outside it was that time of day when, before the war, the street lamps would have begun to glow. Now the twilight faded without interruption. I walked along, thinking what it must be like to be a fugitive from one's own dreams; I had had my share of troubles but, until recently, I had been lucky in sleep. I didn't notice Samuel coming out of the newsagents until he called my name. Although he was due at the unit, he turned around to accompany me to the hostel. We spoke of Tiny Rossiter the anaesthetist's birthday—the patients had given him a boisterous party, with skits and a cake—then I mentioned Neal.

"God damn the dressing station for using tannic acid on him," Samuel said. "He told me a bizarre story."

As he spoke, I caught sight of the unit sister walking ahead of us and tried to make sure that several clear feet separated me from Samuel. Even now that I was fully qualified, my life was controlled by a multitude of rules.

"He wakes up screaming," Samuel continued, "because the dead men in his troop appear in his dreams and tell him he's to blame for their deaths, that he gave the wrong orders. I reminded him that all orders come from HQ—if he'd given the wrong ones he'd be court-martialed—but it made no difference. He kept talking about how the men scream and swear at him, make him look at their injuries and lie down in the mud. I pointed out that these are just figments of his imagination, and he said that didn't matter. The dead men were still speaking the truth."

Samuel gave a little snort, not unlike the sound Lily used to make when confronted with some far-fetched tale. The sister had outstripped us and was lost in the crowd.

"I've asked the chaplain to talk to him," he went on. "Sometimes this kind of nonsense disappears if the right person offers absolution. If that doesn't work, I'll have to get the hospital psychiatrist in for a chat. I can't risk operating while he's in this state." He drew me out of the flow of pedestrians to stand beside a greengrocer's, already closed for the night. In the gloom his brown eyes, normally flecked with gold and topaz, were almost black. "Should I have humoured him, Eva? Pretended to believe in his dreams?"

I pressed my palm to the cold glass of the shop window. "When you told me about the dybbuk," I said, "you seemed to think there might be things some people could see but not others."

"What does the dybbuk have to do with Neal's nightmares?" Samuel's voice was sharp and his dark eyebrows rose.

"Nothing," I said quickly. He had been in the theatre since dawn, I reminded myself, and still had work to do; now was not the moment to discuss dreams and apparitions. "I must go," I added, "or I'll miss dinner." In the dining room Daphne launched into an account of her latest run-in with the night porter, then broke off to ask if I was all right. I pleaded a headache and retreated upstairs. In my room a chair lay on the floor. The maid, I thought; she must have knocked it with her broom and been interrupted before she could pick it up.

The next day as soon as rounds were over I hurried to see Neal. He seemed less startled this time, perhaps because it was broad daylight. "Spring cleaning," I announced, waving my alibi, a yellow duster. "How was breakfast?"

"Dreadful. You wouldn't think," he whispered through his blistered lips, "the cooks could burn porridge every day."

"Are you sleeping better?"

His head gave a little jerk. "No."

I bent over the bed, willing him to confide in me. "Neal, does something trouble you?"

He shrank back, pulling the bedclothes higher. "Nothing troubles me," he said, "nurse."

Against the white of the linen his skin looked even blacker. I stood there, trying to catch his downcast eyes. I had thought I would offer sympathy, tell him I understood about his dreams, perhaps even hint at my own situation, but in the face of his stubborn silence, I did not know how to begin. And what if Neal were to betray me? Some loony nurse, I could hear him saying, some nutter.

Then I took in his ruined features, his hands puffed to twice their normal size; he would be in the unit for months, possibly years. There was plenty of time to win his trust. "Well," I said, wiping the top of his locker, "I'd better get going or Sister will be down on me like a ton of bricks."

Later I would try to tell Samuel about the events of the following afternoon, and it would only lead to more confusion between us. Just before teatime, I was passing Neal's room on my way to the saline baths when the door opened and he appeared in a wheelchair. Over infirmary pyjamas he wore an expensive-looking tartan dressing gown. An older man, dressed in an unfamiliar uniform, was pushing the chair. "Neal," I said, "where are you going?"

The uniformed man—he had a plump, jovial face—answered. "He's off to Loch Lomond to convalesce. Peace and quiet, that's what Neal needs. Time enough for this medical nonsense when he has his strength back."

Neal's face moved in what might have been a smile.

"How long will you be away?" I stepped closer, hoping he might speak for himself. His fine brown hair stirred, as if a breeze were passing. It touched me too. I breathed in a fragrance I recognised, not of medicine or disinfectant but of heather and the sea. As the older man wheeled the chair swiftly forward, I seemed to hear the words, "A long time."

An hour later I was in the linen room, stocking the dressing trolley, when Mollie and another probationer came in, talking in excited voices. The nurse who was serving tea had been unable to rouse Neal Cunningham. Quite unexpectedly, his heart had failed.

"He was a strange fish," said Mollie.

A bandage tangled between my fingers and slipped to the floor. Mollie, laughing, bent to retrieve it. "Back to the sterilizer with this one."

Only the iron routine carried me through the next couple of hours. At the hostel I went directly to my room. The thought that I had seen someone else's companion was overwhelming. I remembered how brisk the older man had been, how good-humoured. What would have happened if I had tried to intervene? Then I remembered Neal's tiny smile and my stupid caution of the day before. I felt sick with disappointment.

Because of Barbara's death we had never celebrated my birthday in April; instead, I shared a cake with Lily in May. Now, somehow, Samuel discovered the actual date and announced that he was taking me to the Royal Hotel, a place I'd heard other nurses talk about but never been to. Later, after I moved to Glenaird and became friends with Anne, it turned out that she and her husband had dined at the Royal that spring on their first visit to Scotland. She couldn't remember the exact date, but it pleased us both to think we might have been there together.

All day on the unit I walked around smiling for no reason, laughing at even the men's stupidest jokes. That evening I allowed myself an extra inch of bathwater and borrowed some of Daphne's precious perfume. Might Samuel at last say something? It was six months since our trip to Troon, and always in our conversations he avoided the topic of the future.

When I came downstairs, my black net rustling, he was waiting in the hall, so handsome in evening clothes that for a moment I didn't recognise him. His face, newly shaved, shone against his pristine shirt, and his dark hair gleamed; he could have just stepped out of a film.

"Eva," he said, bending to kiss my hand, "you look gorgeous."

The walls of the Royal Hotel were lined with sandbags, but inside it was as if the war were already won, the dining room filled with people in evening dress. At our corner table, Samuel produced two packages. The first contained a silk scarf of cornflower blue, the colour that always reminds me of the Little Mermaid and her garden beneath the sea. I draped it round my shoulders and felt the lovely slipperiness against my skin. "Where on earth did you find silk?" I asked.

"I have my sources."

The other gift was a book of Jewish folk tales with an old man in a purple and yellow coat on the cover. Over oxtail soup, Samuel told me the man was a famous king, about to be bamboozled into giving all his money to a beggar.

After the waiter brought our venison in mushroom sauce, I explained my normal birthday ritual. "My father used to say this was an unlucky day long before Barbara died."

Samuel nodded. "My cousin Daniel says that too. April twentieth was the day the Germans went into the Warsaw ghetto."

I had heard of Warsaw, but as with the *Struma* I had not paid attention. Now, watching Samuel's face, I knew better than to ask. I sat, not daring to eat or drink until he spoke again.

"Such gloomy thoughts." He reached out to touch the scarf. "It suits you. I had my brother send it from Montreal. Leo says they're crying out for doctors there, nurses too. Look."

He showed me a set of postcards, coloured views of Toronto, Lake Ontario, Montreal. One card showed a man in a barrel heading for Niagara Falls. As Samuel described the Canadian medical system, the price of land, I felt myself being swept along, like the barrel man. "But Canada is so far away," I said.

"That's what I like about it. After everything that's happened, I'm sick of Europe. Your father would understand."

"Samuel, he has no idea you're a Jew."

He paused, knife and fork raised. "You didn't tell them."

"There was no reason," I stammered.

"Eva, people don't know me if they don't know I'm Jewish. They—" He stopped and I saw his Adam's apple bob as if he were literally swallowing his words. He drank some wine, and when he continued I could hear the restraint in his voice. "Please tell them. I expect to know Lily and David for a long time."

I promised I would, on my next visit. While we waited for dessert, Samuel asked me to dance. As I followed him between the tables, I thought about what he had said: about knowing Lily and David for a long time. It was as if a small piece of the radiance I saw on all sides had bloomed within me. A waltz started. Samuel gathered me to him. I heard him humming under his breath. I remembered David's stories of dancing at the Palais with Barbara. "She sang every tune," he would say.

On the bus to Troon I stared at the scudding clouds and wondered how on earth to bring up Samuel's religion, but almost as soon as I arrived at Ballintyre, Lily provided an opening. The local newspaper had a story about an Ayrshire family who had offered hospitality to Jewish refugees. "Those poor people," she said. "The trouble is, they don't have a country of their own."

"I don't think I mentioned that Samuel's family is Jewish?" I said, as if there was indeed some question.

"We thought as much." Lily reached for the next stitch with her crochet hook; she was making a table mat.

Encouraged, I told her about Canada, how Samuel's brother was there, how he was thinking of going. Everything slowed down. The web of crochet hung motionless from Lily's hands. The tick of the kitchen clock reverberated. Even the fire, with the terrible wartime coal, seemed to burn more slowly.

"Your father's getting old," she said at last. "The war gave him a new lease on life, but he's not strong."

As if on cue, the back door opened and David came in, carrying a coal scuttle. "Eva, I didn't hear you arrive."

He put down the scuttle, kissed my cheek, and went over to the sink. As he washed his hands, I cast a professional eye upon him. He was overweight, stooped, his colour poor, his breathing laboured. I had nursed plenty like him and too often watched them leave the hospital in the worst way.

When my departure drew near, David offered to walk me into town. While he put on his coat and hat, Lily wrapped a jar of precious raspberry jam. "Come again soon," she said, hugging me tight. "We never see you nowadays." Once again, I knew, she was trying to keep me close to home.

As David and I threaded our way among the puddles in the lane, he talked about some difficulty at the insurance office; a company was trying to default on claims. Then he asked about the unit and I described one or two of the men. We were nearing the outskirts of the town when he suggested a visit to Barbara. I tried to conceal my surprise. In the five and a half years since I moved to Glasgow, I had visited the grave only occasionally; David too, I'd assumed, went less often.

At the churchyard I unlatched the gate and, stepping inside, came to an abrupt halt. On the watery surface of the path that led to Barbara's grave writhed a mass of pale pink worms. Beside me, David sighed. "I had her coffin lined with lead," he said. "It's the one thing that lasts."

10

At half a dozen junctures in my life I have longed, with particular passion, for the gift of reading the future. In fact, I suspect I see less of what lies ahead than most people. Tea leaves, spilled salt, black cats, magpies, mirrors, molten lead—none of them speak to me. I have never had the glimpses others claim, often smiling sheepishly: good news about money; oh, my, a tall dark stranger; a journey soon. So I like to think that if I had glimpsed what was coming between Samuel and me, I would never have allowed my admiration for him to turn to love.

The autumn after D-Day, Samuel was asked to take a Maxillo Facial unit to Europe. We spent his last night in Glasgow at the Trattoria and throughout the meal he enthused about his new position. During World War I there had been almost no way to treat men with facial injuries; as a result, many had died of shock or been left severely disfigured. Now these small mobile outfits, nicknamed Max Factors, would treat casualties within hours and prepare them for the reconstructive surgery to come. No more tannic acid, Samuel boasted; he had hopes of constructing a portable saline bath. Trying to set aside my own hopes, I asked questions and listened. He was going to Europe to join the great final push, and it seemed useless to expect a declaration.

At the gates of the hostel he pulled me to him. "Don't forget me, Eva," he whispered.

Next day he was gone, and a few weeks later letters began to arrive in his crabbed writing. He wrote about his patients and, although he signed himself *Love,* he did nothing to nudge our relationship out of the vague romantic terrain where we had spent the last year. When one of the residents invited me to the cinema, I made excuses and, sitting in my room sewing on buttons, wondered why.

As Samuel's unit followed the Allied forces deeper into Europe, his correspondence grew increasingly erratic; there would be no letters for a month, then two or three in a week. Meanwhile, the newspapers carried the first accounts of the Nazi concentration camps. I read them with pained attention. *I still haven't had any Jewish patients,* Samuel wrote, *but I hear terrible rumours.*

Now that the war was ending, there was no longer the same sense of urgency in the infirmary, and the unit, under dour Dr. McFarland, was a very different place. Several of our friends had switched to private nursing, and Daphne was toying with the idea. One afternoon when we were out trying to buy soap, she persuaded me to accompany her to an agency.

The woman behind the desk looked up as we came in. At the sight of our uniforms a smile split her face. "Girls like you," she gushed, "are worth your weight in gold." Then, seeing Daphne's sceptical gaze, added, "Almost."

She flicked through the cards on her desk. "You can take your pick. Mr. Sinclair, he has a hernia. Mr. Morpeth wants a companion for his wife—nerves, he says. We also have some permanent positions. We had an inquiry the other day from a public school for a matron."

The name of the school rang in my ears, a low sweet note; it was in the valley where Barbara had grown up. "Could I have the details of that?" I asked.

"Certainly. A very nice position for someone ladylike."

From the corner of my eye, I saw Daphne smirking. As soon as we were out in the street, she burst into speech. "What a frightful woman! And all those hypochondriacs. Imagine being with some-one's hernia day after day. That's not my idea of nursing." She fulminated all the way to the tearoom.

Shortly after my twenty-fifth birthday, when I hadn't heard from Samuel for almost a month, a crumpled letter arrived. I opened it on the tram to the library.

> *Conditions are dreadful here. Women beg on every street corner. The children are tiny and bowlegged with rickets. The only thing that makes it tolerable is knowing that the war is coming to an end. If it weren't for the politicians, we'd have peace already.*
>
> *Now I can ask you the question that I've been wanting to ever since you rushed to defend me from the woman on the bus. I love you, Eva. Will you marry me? We could go to Canada and start a new life together.*

The vehicle lurched; so did my heart. Sometimes Samuel's hand-writing was hard to read, but he had written the word *marry* with especial clarity. For a couple of stops I was filled with happiness. Then, just as swiftly, happiness ebbed and the companions loomed. Until Samuel knew about them, he could not really ask me to marry him. Their existence was like his being a Jew: a fact so central that without it nothing else about me could be fully understood.

Two days later I was still struggling with my reply when I re-turned from night duty to find Samuel waiting at the door of the hostel. "What are you doing here?" I exclaimed. Before he could answer, I was in his arms.

He had three days' leave which, minus travel time, gave him twelve hours in Glasgow. As we walked down the street he kept tight hold of my hand, and I was too excited to care who saw us. At Tommy's Café he ordered fried bread, black pudding, and beans.

"And you'll be wanting tea," said the waitress.

"Enough tea to float the Armada." He smiled at me. "You don't know how often I've dreamed of breakfasts like this. All we get in the morning is a kind of rusk—the sort of thing they give to pigs and babies."

I laughed, but I did not feel like laughing. Sitting opposite him, I could see that his face was much thinner. His jaw was dark with stubble and his hair straggled dully. More than any single feature, though, I sensed some deeper change; this man would never waltz a sister round the ward.

Over breakfast he described his journey. How calm the Channel was and how everyone on deck sang "The White Cliffs of Dover." I waited for him to talk about the Max Factor unit and their slow ad-vance into Europe, fill in the gaps in his letters, but when I asked about his patients, the state of the towns he'd passed through, his face grew sombre. "Later, Eva," he said, "when we have more time. I've seen things I thought were impossible." For a moment he closed his eyes, and when he opened them again we talked instead about the unit here and his old patients.

We lingered at our table until even the friendly waitress showed signs of impatience. Then we walked to Queen's Park, a few streets away. Before the war the park had been famous for Lily's beloved botanical gardens; now it was filled with rows of vegetables. We sat on a bench near a herbaceous border where the carrot fronds waved young and green. I slipped my arms free of my cape. Beside me Samuel leaned back against the creaking wood.

"Did you get my letter?" he said.

"Yes." With every breath I felt myself approaching the crucial moment, as years before I had run towards the high jump. Soon I would launch myself into the air, and there would be nothing to do but trust that I would clear the bar.

"I owe you an apology," said Samuel. "I know I must have seemed closemouthed during this last year. I couldn't think about my own life until I was sure the war was settled and that I had done whatever I could." He flexed his hands, the same gesture I had seen him make at the White Hart, and I thought of all the stitches he'd sewn, the eyelids and noses and jaws he'd made. "Will you marry me, Eva?"

And now he was looking at me, lips parted, eyes glowing, the old Samuel. "You don't mind," I said, "that I'm not a Jew?"

"Of course not. That would be as bad as you minding that I am." He reached for my hand. "I did wonder if you might convert so that our children would be Jewish, but we can talk about that."

Two elderly men strolled by. The taller of them nodded, and I saw how Samuel and I must look to passersby, both in our uniforms, young, in love. "Samuel, do you remember Neal Cunningham? That boy on the unit who kept everyone awake?"

As I spoke, the air rippled. The woman sat very upright at the end of the bench, her handbag in her lap. During my many meetings with Samuel, she and the girl had never once appeared; it had seemed as if, finally, they knew when they were unwanted. Suddenly I remembered what had happened with Catherine Grant, and my vow of secrecy. But this was different. If Samuel was going to be my husband, I had no choice. I tried to convey this to her in a quick sidelong glance.

Samuel let go of my hand. "Neal Cunningham. What was wrong with him?"

"His face was coated in tannic acid; he died before you could operate. He had nightmares about giving the men in his troop the wrong orders."

"Eva, what does this have to with anything? Were you in love with him?"

"No, no, I only talked to him once." I had meant Neal's story as a prologue to my own. Now dismay at the misunderstanding made me heedless. "I'm trying to tell you that I see people."

Beside me I felt the woman startle, but I was too busy watching Samuel to care. Just as certain words in his letters had resisted all my attempts to decipher them, so now his expression eluded me.

"What do you mean?" he said at last. "People?"

"Well." I fixed my gaze on his boots; they were creased and muddy. "I see—" How dark the mud was. "They're like people, but no one else can see them."

"How long has this been going on?"

"All my life, since I was five or six." Not daring to raise my eyes, I counted the crisscrossings of his laces as I described the companions. Samuel asked what did they do, this woman, this girl, and I explained how they had saved me from the gypsies, dug me out during the air raid. "So," I concluded lamely, "I thought you ought to know."

I had hoped his questions were a sign of belief. Now I realised he had simply been pursuing a diagnosis. "Eva," he said, "many children have imaginary playmates. You were a lonely child and you grew up with two adults who were always talking about a dead woman. No wonder you got confused. But you're an adult. You don't need pretend companions. You have me."

I had been up all night, and the weight of exhaustion fell upon me. An unpleasant metallic taste, like that of the pennies from the bottom of Lily's handbag, flooded my mouth. To my left lay the woman's fury; to my right Samuel's scepticism. All I wanted was to retrieve my words and rest my head on his shoulder.

He was still watching me. "Do you have control over them? Can you summon them at will?"

"I've never tried."

"Because if you can, then you can send them away." He spoke quickly, firmly, as if he had solved a difficult problem.

"Samuel, please. Let's forget about them. We've only got today, and there's so much I want to ask you."

He ignored me. Something else had occurred to him. "Do they ever appear when you and I are together?"

"Occasionally," I said, in a low voice.

"So we might be married, we might be in bed, and you'd be chatting away to your so-called companions." He stared up and down the empty path. "Are they here now?"

I gasped. The woman had seized my arm as she had the night of the air raid. Tighter and tighter she squeezed until I whispered, "No."

Among the carrot fronds two sparrows squabbled. Overhead a plane droned, perhaps returning from France or Belgium.

"Samuel," I went on, "it's not important. How much longer will you be in Europe?"

Without bothering to answer, he stood up and began to pace back and forth in front of the bench. The woman watched for a couple of turns. Then she too rose and stepped into his path. She stood waiting while Samuel walked towards her. He took one step and another, shortening the distance with greedy strides.

I clutched the bench. When only a few feet separated them, I whispered, "Please don't."

The woman gave me a triumphant smile. As Samuel took the final step, she vanished.

He noticed nothing. "You're telling me," he said, "that you regularly talk to ghosts and that it isn't important? If you were a patient, I'd send you to a psychologist or a neurologist."

"You don't have to be mad to see a ghost," I said. I told him about Father Wishart and the ghost of Sir William.

"Wishart is a Catholic priest. Listen, Eva, I don't think you're mad. I think you've indulged a common childhood fantasy to a dangerous degree. But I'm convinced it's within your control. You just have to decide you don't want to see them again, and you won't."

He stopped to bend over me. I had known all along that Samuel was committed to the tangible, to what he could touch and heal, but his ready sympathy, his ability to imagine his most damaged patients as whole, had made me hope he could understand my situation. Now, gazing into his cold brown eyes, I saw that I was wrong. Perhaps when we first met he might have, but not since he had been in Europe. "Can we walk?" I said.

As we strolled around the park, I asked about the Max Factor: Had he been able to implement the saline baths, was it hard to keep dressings and instruments sterile? But Samuel kept returning to the companions. He was not satisfied with my tacit denial. He wanted me to swear that I understood the error of my ways, that I would give them up. Over and over I repeated that this was beyond my power. When that made him angry, I pleaded fatigue, said I had exaggerated, that they were irrelevant.

As the day wore on my despair grew. My confession had rendered every remark suspect: nothing I could say would convince him of my affection. Only in the dark cinema did we escape the spiral of argument. At Glasgow Central, while we waited for his train, Samuel told me he would not write. "I've offered you my life," he said. "It's up to you, whether you want me."

That morning he had embraced me as if I were all that he needed to be whole. Now, on the station platform, he raised his arms, not to draw me close but to keep me at a distance; a stranger might have taken us for casual acquaintances.

Samuel's train left at eight, and I was on duty at nine. The night was an endless series of small difficulties. The staff nurse had a headache, a sergeant complained that his Tobruk plaster pinched. By the time I returned to the hostel, I was too tired even for breakfast.

Hours later I woke with a feeling akin to anger, not with the woman—she was just doing what she'd always done, trying to keep me to herself—but with Samuel. If he loved me, he should try to understand. He should be grateful to the companions for saving my life. While I slept two chairs had overturned. Beneath one of them I found the piece of paper from the agency with the address of the school: Mr. Frank Thornton, Headmaster, Victoria College, Glenaird.

11

Mr. Thornton invited me for an interview by return of post. Later I learned I was the only applicant for the position. With Daphne's help, I put together a respectable outfit, borrowing a hat from one nurse and a handbag from another, and retraced the journey Barbara had made nearly thirty years before. One of the masters met me at Perth Station and drove me the ten miles to the school. As we came over the final rise into the valley, I felt I was seeing a landscape I had always known. The rough fields and woods stretched down to the river, and on the far side the bare hills rolled away in either direction as far as the eye could see. This is where Barbara grew up, I thought, and beneath the overcast sky everything that lay within my gaze glittered.

Sitting in Mr. Thornton's oak-panelled study, I seemed possessed of an unusual fluency, and on our tour of the school sanatorium I found it easy to ask appropriate questions. Still, when Daphne asked how the interview had gone, I shrugged and said so-so. The next day I volunteered for all the overtime available; I worked early and late and at night fell into bed too tired to think.

A fortnight later a second letter arrived from Glenaird and I carried it around, rustling in my pocket, for an entire day before opening it. "The school matron," Mr. Thornton wrote, "is an essential part of our community and a force for good in the lives of boys and masters alike. We hope very much that you will accept the position."

I had not heard from Samuel since he left Glasgow, nor had I been able to bring myself to write to him. That night after supper I sat down at my desk. Several of Samuel's patients were still in the unit, and I started with the simple part, an account of Raymond's wrists, Duncan's eyelids. Then "I fear we're not suited. You want to go to Canada, and I could never leave my father and Aunt Lily. They're the only family I have."

For a long while I sat holding my pen, looking at those three abrupt sentences; nothing more occurred to me. But as I folded the letter into the envelope, everything I liked about Samuel rushed back. I remembered the pleasure he had taken in keeping me out until the last minute of curfew. I remembered the evening we had played charades at the unit, how the patients had cheered his young Lochinvar. Suddenly I was convinced I was making a terrible mistake. I could ask the companions to stay away. They would understand. And if I promised to go to Canada eventually, surely Samuel would agree to live in Scotland for now. I was about to tear up my letter, and write a refusal instead to Mr. Thornton, when Daphne knocked on my door with cocoa.

"Here," she said, handing me a cup. "Am I interrupting?"

"No, I was just trying to write to Samuel."

Daphne took up her customary perch on the edge of the bed. "So"—she blew on her cocoa—"forgive me for being nosy, but what happened? You've been awfully glum since his visit."

For a fleeting moment, as she eyed me over her cup, I thought of telling the truth. Then I remembered my last attempt and fell back on Canada, an excuse which made Daphne bob in sympathy; she had often said she could never leave her Glasgow family.

In bed that night my dreams were as turbulent as if I were contemplating murder. I smelled again the boy's beery breath; I heard the explosion that had trapped me in the doorway of the haberdasher's. Meanwhile the furniture flew round the room. Between dreams I glimpsed my clothes dancing.

First light showed my desk empty except for the letter to Samuel; a stamp had been affixed, not by me. In my dressing gown, I carried the envelope downstairs and dropped it into the box.

Lily and David both greeted the news of the school with delight. Although I would be farther away, I would have three months' holiday a year, and going to Barbara's birthplace gave the plan an inevitable legitimacy. In July I quit the infirmary and returned to Troon. I had not been home for more than a week since I left, and Lily was determined to treat me as a guest. "Rest. Take it easy," she kept saying. "You deserve a holiday."

She did not understand that I would happily have scrubbed the floor from dawn to dusk to keep at bay the thoughts that breached too easily my idle hours. As the days passed, I found myself growing more, not less, preoccupied with Samuel. When I thought that I had given him up for the companions, I cursed my own stupidity. Then I cursed them. They had followed me back to Troon but, as if sensing my anger, kept their distance.

The Saturday after my return, David and I went to visit Barbara. The results of the general election had been announced the previous week, and the impromptu party at the hostel had also been my farewell. Now, as we ambled down the lane, David remarked how glad he was he had lived to see a Labour government in power.

I told him Samuel had said it would be the best thing to happen since the repeal of the Poor Laws.

David smiled. "I don't know if I'd go that far, but the situation after the last war was a scandal. At least this government cares about working people."

At the grave, dandelions had sprung up and the grass was littered with leaves and beech mast. As I bent to retrieve a branch, he apologised. "I'm not as spry as I used to be."

"Never mind. I'll come back on Monday and tidy up."

He was staring at the stone. "Barbara and I talked about Glenaird so often, I can still picture the valley. We meant to go there after you were born. I suppose in a way we are."

I gazed at the map of lichen that spread across my mother's name and tried to hold back tears.

The end of July brought David's seventy-third birthday. Lily had hoarded eggs and sugar to bake a cake, and she and I joined together to give him a new fishing rod. It was too long to wrap. Instead, I wound nasturtiums and morning glories from the handle to the tip.

"My goodness," David said. "You'll make me into an angler yet."

He mimed a cast, and the orange and blue flowers swayed as if the rod had magically bloomed in his hands; for a moment he was young again. Then he began to wind the reel, and I saw with dismay how stiffly his fingers moved.

Lily carried in the cake with seven big candles and three little ones. "Don't forget to wish," I said.

He paused, lips parted. "I wish——"

"You mustn't tell," I interrupted. "Else it won't come true."

He closed his eyes and blew out the ten candles in a single swoop. Lily and I clapped.

The next day was unusually warm. A haze hung over the meadows, and even the blackbirds were silent. After lunch, David announced that he was going fishing. Lily made him a thermos of tea, and I lined the bottom of his basket with long grass. "I'll be providing the supper tonight," he joked.

I helped Lily with the dishes, and together we made a batch of scones; then she shooed me away. I carried my book, *The Mill on the Floss,* out to the bench in the garden. The bees were buzzing in the roses. On the page the print too seemed to buzz as Maggie Tulliver floated down the river.

"Eva," said a low, insistent voice. "Eva."

I sat up, startled. The garden was empty, save for a couple of sparrows in the apple tree. A dream, I thought, some remnant of the book, but I did not go back to sleep. I struggled to my feet and went inside to get a drink of water.

I was at the sink, drying my hands, when Lily appeared. "There you are," she said. "I was wondering if you'd fetch David. Tea will be ready soon, and he doesn't like to rush."

I took the path through the woods. Beneath the trees it was dark and cool, a pleasant relief after the heat of the garden, but instead of slowing my pace I walked faster and faster. By the time I emerged onto the riverbank, I was trotting.

At first glance, David appeared to be standing knee-deep in the water, leaning against the steep bank. As I came closer I saw that he had collapsed. His left hand still held the rod. It floated before him, bobbing in the current.

"I felt a bit funny," he whispered.

"Father," I said urgently. Beneath my fingers his pulse fluttered.

I half rose, searching the riverbank for other fishermen, in vain. All the men were helping with the harvest. I did not know what to do. I must fetch a doctor, but at any moment David might slide down into the water.

"We have to get you out of the river," I said.

I stepped behind him and slid my hands under his shoulders. I was used to moving patients, balancing their weight with my own. Now I tugged, I heaved, but all my straining did not budge my father. If anything, he sank a little lower.

"Eva," he murmured, "you'll do yourself an injury."

I let go and stood up. My thoughts jostled frantically: to go, to stay, to go. Then into my mind came an image of the girl and the woman. "Please help me," I begged. "Please."

Once more I bent to grasp David's shoulders. There was nothing in the world save the need to move him to safety. I shut my eyes, dug in my heels, and leaned back with all my might.

For a few seconds he remained obdurate. Then I felt him shift, a hair's breadth, one inch, two. Opening my eyes, I saw two men in old-fashioned army uniforms, kneeling on either side of my father, and in the river stood a third, lifting his legs. David was free of the water. Led by the woman, we carried him over the grass and propped him against a beech tree. As noiselessly as they had appeared, the men retreated into the woods; beside me the girl helped to loosen David's collar, remove his waterlogged boots.

"He needs a doctor," said the woman, and she and the girl too were gone.

David stared at me. Before he could try to speak, I said, "You stay here. I'll fetch Dr. Pyper."

"That's not necessary." He spoke with long pauses, as if he must search for each word in crowded rooms.

"I just meant I'll find someone who has a car." I bent to kiss his cheek and felt the bristles; he had shaved carelessly that morning.

I walked until I was out of sight. Then, heedless of the uneven ground, I sprinted. As I neared the road, I heard the sound of a vehicle approaching and, with a final burst of speed, I leapt up the bank and hurled myself into its path.

The car stopped a few yards away. Nora Blythe, as upright and efficient as she had been seven years before when she tried to make me into a secretary, opened the door. I spluttered out a couple of sentences. "I'll fetch the doctor," she said.

I ran back the way I had come. Let him be alive, I prayed. Let him be alive. As soon as I saw him, beneath the tree, I knew that my wish had been granted. I stopped to catch my breath and straighten my clothes. When I thought I could appear calm, I hurried towards him.

"I met Miss Blythe on the road. She's bringing help."

"Good." Even the single syllable seemed to exhaust him.

I brought my face close to his, so that his eyes might dwell upon my countenance, and began to talk. Often at the infirmary I chatted to patients as they came out of the anaesthetic or when I was changing a dressing, but that was different. Now I spoke with desperate fluency, as if David's life depended upon my words, as if all that anchored him to the world was the thin cord of my conversation.

"Do you remember coming here when I was little? Before I started at Miss MacGregor's, we would walk down in the evening. You would lean on the bridge and ask if I wanted a peppermint. I had to guess which pocket they were in. Then I put in my hand to see if I was right. There were little shreds of tobacco in the seams, and afterwards my hands smelled of tobacco and peppermint."

Above our heads the canopy of beech leaves trembled; the sunlight touched David's face.

"We used to go fishing on Saturdays," I continued. "I brought my net and jam jar and you made me go downstream. I watched you wade out into the water, like a giant in your seven-league boots. There was that lovely hissing sound as you cast. The part I didn't like was when you caught a fish. I don't think you enjoyed that either. You always hit them on the head immediately."

David sighed.

"Once we came in the autumn when the salmon were running: so many fish the water was shaking with silver. All along the banks, men were practically shoveling them out. You watched for a minute and turned away. Later you told Lily it was a massacre, like Passchendaele. She said you were too softhearted. I expect she was cross we weren't getting a salmon."

I put my hand on his forehead. His eyes, which only the day before had been blue as the morning glories, were dim, and I wondered if anything reached him. Just then I heard voices. Miss Blythe emerged from beneath the trees, followed by Dr. Pyper, breathing hard but casting a spell of reassurance, and the Tyler brothers carrying a stretcher.

In his hospital bed, hour by hour David grew weaker. He was slipping out of life as inexorably as he might, but for the companions, have slipped into the water. Lily and I sat with him. It was during the second night, when I had persuaded her to go and lie down, that David said, "I want to tell you my wish."

"Your wish?"

"For my birthday. I wished for your happiness."

Beneath the warm flesh of his chest I felt his tremulous heart beat. If I could, I would have given him my organs, my life's blood. In lieu of those impossible offerings I poured out what I had: love, gratitude.

"Something happened by the river," he said.

"Yes." A nurse padded by in the corridor. "The companions moved you to safety." I stroked his chest, wanting him to know and understand before it was too late. "They've been with me all my life."

The faintest of smiles passed over David's face. "Maybe Barbara sent them."

"Maybe she did." At once the idea seemed right. My mother had sent back emissaries from that far country. Then I told him everything I had tried to tell Samuel, including what had come of my attempts to confide. "I wanted to send them away," I said. "I'm so glad I didn't." While I spoke David's eyes fell shut. I leaned forward to wipe his face. I found myself remembering our last visit to Barbara's grave. Surely no day had passed without my father thinking of my mother.

Lily and I emerged from the hospital to discover that victory over Japan had been declared. Ballintyre was probably the only house for miles around that did not fling open the curtains and turn on the lights. The funeral the next day was dominated by Aunt Violet. Her train from Edinburgh was late and she hurried down the aisle of Saint Cuthbert's just as the organ started. In the high-pitched voice Mrs. Nicholson had imitated, she launched into the opening hymn.

Afterwards she played the part of chief mourner. "A tragedy," she kept saying, "but at least he didn't suffer." When the guests had gone, she raised her veil to glare at Lily. "The undertaker told me we'd lined the coffin with lead. I don't know what you were thinking of. Every penny counts now."

"It was what he would have wanted," said Lily quietly.

We went to Mr. Laing's office for the reading of the will. It was very brief; everything was to be divided between Lily and me. Violet asked how much that was, and Mr. Laing said to the best of his knowledge less than five hundred pounds. I had given no thought to the practical consequences of David's death; now Mr. Laing made clear that Lily could not remain at Ballintyre. Even if she had the money, the lease was in David's name, and the owner was anxious to repossess. "So, Miss McEwen," he said awkwardly, "I'm afraid you'll have to move."

"No," I exclaimed. "It's our home."

"Hush, Eva," said Violet. She turned to Mr. Laing. "Lily can stay with me. We're neither of us as young as we used to be, and I could do with the help."

"That sounds grand," said Mr. Laing.

I looked at Lily, waiting for her to disagree, but she sat clutching her gloves. Overnight she had shrunk from being the mistress of Ballintyre to a poor relation, a burden to herself and others.

Next day, as if by prior arrangement, Lily and I rose early and, after a hasty breakfast, left the house, where Violet lay sleeping, and headed down the lane. The soft, tearing sound of the cows grazing in the nearby fields accompanied our conversation.

"Can't we find a way to stay?" I asked.

"You heard what Mr. Laing said. We lived on David's pension. That would pass to his widow, not to me. Besides, old Buchanan is very keen to get us out. We've been paying this tiddly rent for ages."

"But living with Aunt Violet . . ."

"I don't see, Eva, what choice I have."

Lily's voice was thin as a reed, and at once I felt ashamed. After all, I had no home to offer. "Anyway," she continued, "I'm not sure I'd want to stay here by myself. David did try to warn me. Last spring he said he worried about what was going to happen—"

A shrill cry broke her words. Thirty yards ahead in the branches of an ash tree a magpie dipped and swayed, its plumage glinting in the sunlight. As we drew closer I could see the shining rim around each dark eye.

"Remember the old rhyme?" Lily asked.

Almost unthinkingly I recited:

"One for sorrow, two for mirth,
Three for a wedding, four for a birth.
Five's a christening, six a dearth,
Seven's heaven, eight is hell,
And nine's the devil his ane sel'."

"When you were born," said Lily, "the midwife saw six magpies fighting in the garden."

"I know. You chided her for being superstitious."

With a final shriek the bird swooped over the hedge. We walked on. "David used to think you would marry," Lily said, "and that would solve everything. After you brought Samuel home, he got his hopes up."

I turned to her, amazed—hadn't she been opposed to my marrying Samuel?—but she was looking at the hawthorn. The flowers that year were especially creamy and abundant.

Later that afternoon, when Violet and Lily were going through the china, I sat down to write to Samuel. I began with my father's death, and then I found the words that I thought would please him. He was right: I had conjured up the companions out of my lonely childhood. If we were married, I would never see them again. As for Canada, I would be happy to go so long as Lily could come too.

As I wrote, I kept glancing over my shoulder. I thought of David's rescue, and my hand shook so, I could barely pen the sentences. Then I thought of Lily, hunched in her seat at Mr. Laing's, and I went on. Surely the companions would understand that I was only trying to correct the mistake I had made by mentioning them in the first place. "I don't mean any of this," I whispered. "I'll just keep you secret, like I do from Lily."

Ten days later I came down to breakfast to see an envelope by my place. At last. Another step, and I saw that it was my own letter. Next to Samuel's name someone had scrawled: *Not known.* After a moment, I recognised the writing. Only three months ago the same hand had written *Marry me.*

I sat down, oblivious to Lily's offers of tea and toast but accepting both. Today we were sorting the linen. "David kept the bits and pieces Barbara brought from Glenaird. You'll want those, won't you?"

"Yes," I said. Then I noticed she was watching me with a strange mixture of earnestness and embarrassment. "What is it?"

She shook her head. "Before you came downstairs I was sitting here at the table with the place opposite, and it was as if I were waiting for David. I could hear you moving around and I was sure it was him."

"I feel the same. I keep thinking he's just stepped out to feed the hens or see if his cabbages have grown. I don't want to stop. There's plenty of time to be sensible."

I gazed at Lily and she returned my gaze. Through the open window came the rustling of the wind in the apple tree, a bird cheeping, the distant clatter of a tractor in the meadow, and, in the midst of all these other sounds, a creaking noise—as if someone had opened and closed the garden gate—and, even more faintly, the crunch of gravel. We sat there, not moving, hardly breathing, as David passed by.

Part III

MY MOTHER'S
VALLEY

12

One of the first stories I told Anne about Samuel concerned the would-be suicide. A young man, a navigator, whose jaw Samuel had been rebuilding for six months, had tried to slash his wrists but was foiled by the pedicle graft growing between his right arm and his mouth. When Samuel heard the news, he rushed to the unit. "For God's sake," he scolded the navigator, "don't kill yourself until the pedicle is established. It needs another fortnight at least." The two of them had burst out laughing and, later, so did Anne and I.

But that was hours, days, weeks after I arrived at the school. That first day when I climbed down from the train at Perth Station, I could not imagine ever laughing again. Mrs. Thornton, the headmaster's wife, had come to meet me. Her shelflike bosom and massive green hat reminded me of Aunt Violet, and at first she seemed just as stern. In a matter of minutes she had organised a porter to load my suitcases into the car, and we were driving with erratic speed through the town and into the countryside. For the last few weeks, as Lily and I emptied Ballintyre, the sounds of harvesting had filled the echoing rooms. Here, a hundred miles north, the stooks of corn still waited to be gathered in. While Mrs. Thornton pointed out landmarks—Huntingtower Castle, the Ochil Hills—I wondered what on earth I had done, coming to such an isolated place.

"Lovely," I said flatly.

I felt her quick glance. "When Frank and I came here from London," she said, "I cried every day. Now I wouldn't live anywhere else. I hope you'll come to feel that way too, Miss McEwen. Oh, my goodness."

The car swerved, and I thought there must be something in the road.

"My dear, I forgot to say how sorry I am about your father."

"Thank you," I said. It was a relief to hear anyone, even a stranger, offer sympathy, and for the rest of the journey I was able to pay attention to her conversation. At the school, she handed me over to the Polish couple who took care of the sanatorium. "Their English is not good," she warned, "but they have hearts of gold."

In the kitchen Mr. and Mrs. Plishka stood side by side, stout and smiling, like Tweedledum and Tweedledee. "How do you do?" they said in unison. Mrs. Plishka did the cooking and cleaning, Mr. Plishka the heavy work. As soon as Mrs. Thornton left, they introduced me to the most important member of the household, Tizzie. The calico cat nuzzled my hand. "She likes," said Mrs. Plishka, and I caught the gleam of a gold tooth.

I had not seen the matron's flat when I came for my interview— the headmaster had offered some vague, awkward excuse—and now

I climbed the stairs and wandered, marvelling, from room to room: a bedroom, a sitting room, a bathroom, and a kitchen, all for my sole use. From the sitting room window, I had a view across the cricket pitch to the main school. On the flagpole above the clock tower fluttered the white cross of Saint Andrew, and beyond, on the far side of the river, rose the bare hills.

I had arrived the day before the boys, and once I had unpacked and organised my possessions, there was little to do. Mrs. Lancaster, my predecessor, had left the ward and surgery immaculate. On the desk lay a sheaf of notes. "The toilet window sticks, especially in winter." "Do not leave the sitting room door open. Tizzie will sneak in." "Dr. Singer inclined to be chatty." Next to the notes a book recorded the details of every patient, over and over the same minor ailments: cuts, sprains, colds, measles, chicken pox. In ten years not a single death.

The following day brought a flurry of introductions. Soon after nine Dr. Singer came by, and I invited him in for tea. A lanky young man with reddish hair, his singsong accent reminded me of Bernard; later I learned he too had been born near Oban. At first our stilted conversation seemed to belie Mrs. Lancaster's description, but when he knocked the begonia off the table—he was praising the view—and saw that I wasn't upset, he grew more voluble. His practise was based in a village halfway between the school and Perth, and many of his patients lived on remote farms. "It's hard," he said, "having no colleagues." His ears reddened, almost to match his hair, as he confessed the muddle he'd made of his first case of diabetes.

I was still washing our teacups when the next visitor arrived. A woman in a pleated skirt and blue cardigan, looking scarcely older than a schoolgirl, appeared at my sitting room door, her arms full of roses. As Anne introduced herself, the fragrance of the flowers drifted towards me, and briefly I was back at Ballintyre, where year after year David had tended his roses with tea leaves and ashes.

While I chose a vase, Anne gazed around the room. "You've made it so much nicer," she said. "Mrs. Lancaster kept it like a dentist's waiting room. I am glad she's gone. I knew she'd say something dire when she learned I was expecting."

At this last sentence dimples appeared in both cheeks. I offered congratulations. With her wide eyes and bobbing manner, Anne reminded me of a wren. She told me she and her husband, Paul, had come to the school the year before; he taught mathematics; only three of the other masters were married. "As for single women," she added, "you'll have to be careful we don't gobble you up."

I tried to smile—spinster, spinster—but my face must have betrayed me. Anne retreated into practical matters: where to buy stamps, how to get to Perth. Before she left, she drew me a map of the short distance to her house.

That night, sitting by the fire, I was surprised to realise that I longed for the companions. I had not seen them since the day by the river. Going to Glasgow, I had hoped to be rid of them. Now what I dreaded was abandonment. I had lost David, lost Samuel; was I to lose them too? "I'm sorry," I said. "You know I only wanted to help Lily."

In the Plishkas' part of the house wireless music flared, then muffled again. The curtains hung motionless, the blue vase sat on the mantelpiece, the begonia squatted on the table. Nothing moved.

The first week at the san was the exact opposite, medically speaking, of my experiences at the infirmary. A steady stream of boys came to the surgery, claiming nothing more serious than coughs and upset stomachs. In return I offered spoonfuls of medicine and small jokes. Mostly I diagnosed nerves about the start of school. Certainly that was true for the skinny suntanned boy who arrived one rainy morning with a badly gashed knee; he had slipped running to class.

"What's your name?" I said, fetching the iodine.

"Scott. I'm a new boy."

"Like me."

As I cleaned the wound, Scott squirmed—not, he explained, from pain but in fear of being late. When I promised a note for the master, he grew still and began to tell me about his summer holidays. His days on the beach at Elgin sounded much like those I had once passed with Mrs. Nicholson's children.

After Scott left and I had written him up in the surgery log, I found myself standing at the window, watching the rain, close to tears: no cinema, no shops, no library, no trams, and no patients who really needed me. Worst of all, no Samuel. For a few days after David collapsed on the riverbank, I had believed that my peculiar choices made sense. Now I could no longer remember why telling Samuel the truth had seemed so important. And what had prevented me, after my botched attempt, from simply lying to make amends? I pictured his face when he first caught sight of me on the evening of my birthday, how he had held me as we danced.

I fetched my coat and walked the short distance to Anne's house. Fidgeting on her doorstep, I tried to think of an excuse for my visit, but at the sight of me her dimples appeared. "Eva," she exclaimed. In an instant, she had me seated by the fire.

"I hope I'm not interrupting," I said feebly.

"Not at all. I was just looking at some skirts, to see if they could be let out. Are you good at sewing?"

"Dreadful."

She laughed, a surprisingly throaty sound that again made me think of a small bird. "I suppose living in Glasgow, there was no need with all those shops and tailors."

"Actually I swapped with my friend Daphne. I cleaned her shoes or went to the library in exchange for mending."

"We could do that. It's none of my business," she went on, "but I can't help wondering why you took this job. I mean Glenaird isn't exactly the centre of the universe."

I told her the parts of the story that could be told: not Samuel, not yet, but how my grandparents had worked at the Grange, and how Barbara at the age of fifteen had been sent to Troon as a house-maid, and about David and Lily and losing Ballintyre.

"Oh, how awful," said Anne. She asked if I still had relatives in the valley, and I shook my head. The flu epidemic that took Barbara had also carried away her parents; her surviving uncles and aunts had passed on in the twenties.

Anne nodded sympathetically and bent to tend the fire. "The Grange is only half a mile away," she said. "The Rintouls live there, but they don't mind people walking through the grounds." Then she confided the shadow in her life: her brother, Oliver, had been in the final stages of the Italian campaign and had come home utterly changed. "He wanders around like a beggar. The neighbours don't recognise him."

"It's early days," I said. I described some of the remarkable recoveries I'd seen—the man who, after a month of silence, greeted me one morning; the sailor, so fearful of water he refused to bathe, who now swam with pleasure—and she seemed comforted.

As I walked back to the san, I started making bets. If I held my breath for eight steps, the furniture would have moved. If I held my breath for ten, one of the companions would be there. But when I opened the door of my sitting room, everything was exactly where I had left it.

On the next dry afternoon, I asked Mrs. Plishka for directions and walked up the main road to look at the Grange. Larger than Larch House, it was built of the same grey granite. A copper beech, like the one by Barbara's grave, grew near the front door, and from the first large branch hung a swing. So this was where Barbara had spent her childhood, had polished the brasses and seen her future husband. I longed to look through one of the dark windows, but as I stepped closer, somewhere inside a dog began to bark forlornly.

I followed the drive up the gentle hill. Around the bend, I came upon an immensely tall conifer with spongy reddish bark. I was standing looking at it, wondering what kind of tree this was, when a pain stabbed my side. Not appendicitis, I thought, paging through a textbook; not kidneys.

"It's a California redwood." The girl stepped from behind the trunk.

"You're here." I was so pleased I almost embraced her

"In California they have whole forests of these trees. Some of them are big enough for a car to drive through the trunk."

She watched me with her bluebell eyes. The pain throbbed and was gone. "How did it get here?" I asked.

"The first owner of the Grange went to America and brought several back. This was the only one to survive."

"You seem to know an awful lot about it." The girl tossed her braids and began to edge away. "Do you want to go for a walk?" I added quickly.

"Not today. You should go home too." With a final flick of her braids, she stepped behind the tree.

As I headed back to the san, I noticed neither the light on the hills nor the sheep in the fields. The girl was here, and surely the woman had come too. My loneliness blew away, like dandelion seeds in the wind.

A few days, perhaps a week later, I was at my sitting room window, drawing the curtains, when I saw a dog on the cricket pitch. No, not a dog, a fox trotting across the dewy grass, head held low. I had last glimpsed one with David, in the lane by Ballintyre. How pleased he would be when I told him. Then, as the animal disappeared behind the pavilion, the sorrow returned, as keen as the day by the river.

"He was very glad you were coming here," the woman said. She was standing behind me.

She smiled and seemed to understand that I could not speak.

"When we lived near Fort William," she continued, "a family of foxes had their earth at the back of our cottage. In the evenings we would watch the cubs play."

"You lived near Fort William?" For a moment I was so startled that even my sadness was forgotten.

"My husband was working on the railway as an engineer. Later, of course, we moved to Troon." She pointed to the door. "I think you have a visitor."

Mrs. Plishka, a dab of flour on her red cheek, held out a plate. "Scones," she said. "For breakfast, with honey."

From then on the companions came often, singly and together, and were more forthcoming than they had ever been. The girl knew not only about the redwood but where to find the last blackberries and the best chestnuts. The woman spoke of her husband and sons; for their first anniversary her husband had made her a stainless-steel toast rack. "Dear man," she said. "It held six slices. He couldn't understand why I laughed and laughed. Such an unromantic gift."

As the weeks passed I gradually grew accustomed to the rhythms of my new life, the awkward boys, the lack of bustle, my pleasant flat. Happily, Anne and I fell into friendship. Such was the nature of the infirmary that I had never before had a married friend, and sometimes I longed to ask what was it like, having a man so close all the time, but there was a delicacy about Anne that forbade intrusions. One Saturday in early October, she suggested a walk to the nearest village, on the far side of the valley. By road it was over four miles; using the footbridge across the river less than two. "I'll show you the pub," she said, "and we can look at your mother's school."

The afternoon was so clear and still that, as we descended the stairs to the river, I could hear each separate leaf falling in the woods around us. We crossed the bridge and followed the track up the hill, between fields of sheep. Anne asked about Barbara: Had she been good at school?

"Not especially." I tried to recall David's stories. "She had to stand in the corner for a whole afternoon because she got caught carving her initials on her desk. And she left when she was fifteen."

"I used to write things on my desk but I don't remember carving. That sounds very enterprising."

The village was a mere few dozen houses clustered around the school, the church, and the pub. A young woman, face puffy, hair dishevelled, answered our knock at the schoolhouse door. Anne and I exchanged guilty glances; she had clearly been asleep. I apologised for disturbing her and explained our errand.

Still yawning, the teacher fetched the key. Inside, while Anne questioned her—How many children? Did she teach languages?—I pretended to study a map of the Holy Land.

"Come to me," I whispered, closing my eyes. I imagined the photograph of Barbara that hung above my bed coming to life. But when I looked around, I saw only Anne and the teacher.

"Maybe we can find her initials," said Anne. "How long have these desks been here?"

"Since well before my time." The teacher had sat down at the front, as if about to commence a lesson.

Every desk I examined was a mass of initials, swearwords, caricatures. I was gazing despairingly at a stick figure when a slight noise caught my attention. Near the window the lid of a desk was rising slowly into the air. Fortunately, Anne was engrossed in another desk, the teacher oblivious. I hurried to press down the lid.

Amid the dense tangle the initials emerged, the *B* nicely chubby, the *M* not quite finished. I ran my finger over the letters. In them I glimpsed my mother, not the misty, demure woman of the photograph, whom I had tried to summon a few minutes earlier, but the lively girl of David's stories—good at party games, able to recite the whole of "Tam O'Shanter," a terrible cook. Already, I thought, I was six years older than she had ever been.

When I showed Anne, she clapped her hands. "I knew we could find it," she said, and I was touched by her belief.

Outside the school, we thanked the teacher and were about to retrace our steps when a man emerged from the pub, bareheaded. "Anne," he called, and walked towards us, smiling. He bent to kiss her cheek, and she made introductions.

"Eva McEwen, Matthew Livingstone."

"Like the explorer," he remarked, just as the same thought crossed my mind. "I wanted to ask your permission to visit one of your patients, Douglas Best."

Later it was to seem a good omen that almost the first thing I noticed about Matthew was his owl-like glasses, similar to those Barbara had worn. His hair was the shade of brown that fair children often have as adults. I told him he could visit the san any time between two and five. Then he offered us a lift, but Anne said no, we were on our constitutional. As we headed out of the village, I asked what Matthew taught.

"English and first-form Latin. He came to the school a year before us and was friendly from the start. He helped me with the garden, and he's a great games player: cards, consequences. Rumour has it he came north to escape a broken engagement."

"Really?" I said, my attention caught by the coincidence. Not that Samuel and I had ever been engaged.

Back at the san, Lily's weekly letter was waiting. She enclosed a photograph she'd discovered among David's papers: the three of us picnicking on the beach one summer afternoon before the war. David was smiling broadly, holding a sandwich; I had my skirts hitched up from paddling, and even Lily, although she wore a hat, had taken off her shoes. Gazing at our sunlit faces, I yearned to be back in that time and place.

In the unit the trickiest cases were the men who displayed photographs of themselves, as if they could, miraculously, be reunited with their former features. Here, doctor, they would say, you can see my eyes were always a little close together; my nose did have a bit of a bump. I recall the awful day Archie's fiancée came to visit. It was shortly after Samuel had operated, pulling a flap of skin down from Archie's forehead to form new nostrils, and we were all optimistic that this time the graft would take. But Cecily had sat by his bed, sobbing—"I can't, Archie. I just can't"—until the staff nurse turned on the wireless, full volume.

Later, after Cecily left, sniffling away on her high heels, I approached, thinking to offer the inadequate solace of tea or the paper. Without a word, Archie held out a photograph. A handsome young man in RAF uniform gazed up at me. Cecily's new beau, I assumed, the man who had tempted her away from Archie; then I saw the inscription: *Darling Cecily, with much love from your very own high flyer, Archie.* I was still looking back and forth between the man in the picture and the man in the bed when Archie plucked the photograph from my hand and, in one swift movement, tore it in two.

On Monday Matthew arrived at the san with a grammar book and settled down with Douglas Best. "Do you know what the possessive is?"

"No, sir." The boy shook his head emphatically.

They worked for an hour, until I brought the tea tray. "Now," said Matthew, "what about a game?" In a few minutes he had organised Best, the two other boys in the ward, himself, and me into gin rummy.

The following week he invited me to see *Major Barbara* in Perth; he had wangled an extra allowance of petrol. I accepted his invitation unthinkingly. Romance had become as foreign to me as the phrases the Plishkas tossed back and forth; besides, who else would he ask? The two school secretaries were cut from the same cloth as Nora Blythe, and the only other single women were the girls working in the kitchens.

I had last been to the theatre with Samuel, and as the usher showed us to our seats I could not help wondering where he was, whether he ever thought of me. Then Matthew drew my attention to the fresco on the ceiling. "That cherub in the corner looks a bit like Best," he said.

The lights dimmed, and soon, almost in spite of myself, I was smiling at Barbara's attempts to bully her family into good behaviour. Beside me, Matthew laughed heartily.

Afterwards at the George Hotel he ordered beer, and in a moment of daring I asked for a whisky mac, Daphne's favourite tipple. We secured a window table, with a view across the River Tay. Matthew remarked that this was the first time he had been to the hotel since the blackout ended. We had the usual conversation about where we'd each spent the war. He had taught in a school in his hometown of Stoke-on-Trent. "Bad eyes," he said, indicating his spectacles as if I might have missed them.

I wanted to ask why he had come north. It was a natural question but not one I thought I could ask naturally. I sipped my drink.

"Did Major Barbara remind you of anyone?" he said.

"No."

"Are you sure?" He puffed out his chest.

"Mrs. Thornton."

"She who knows what's best for you, better than you know yourself." We both laughed.

Back at the san, only the hall lights were on. The Plishkas had retired for the night and my patients, when I went to check, were sleeping peacefully. For a moment, standing at the foot of the dark ward, I longed for the infirmary. Even on the quietest night, someone had always been awake, eager for conversation. Then I opened my sitting room door and found the woman seated by the hearth.

"Hello, I'm watching Tizzie sleep." She pointed to the other armchair, where the cat lay, paws twitching.

I slipped off my coat and scooped Tizzie onto my lap. "I went to see *Major Barbara*."

"Matthew is a nice man, don't you think?"

I stared; it was so unlike her to offer this kind of opinion. "I hardly know him," I said at last.

The woman gave a little frown. "What about the play?"

"I liked it, though I think they made it too easy to laugh at Barbara." I scratched Tizzie's head. "I didn't even notice that she has the same name as my mother."

"I can't imagine your mother ordering people about." The woman was gazing at the feathery ashes.

I remembered what David had said in the hospital. "Did you know Barbara?"

She nodded.

"Can you tell me about her?"

The woman stepped over to the mantelpiece, where Barbara's blue jug had the place of honour. Delicately, she touched the rim. "You know her by being here, by walking these roads and seeing what she saw. You should let that content you."

Alone, I carried the protesting Tizzie out to the corridor. She stalked off, tail waving. The woman had known Barbara. In the midst of so much loss, here was one small gain.

13

Christmas brought three weeks' holiday. Anne and Paul were staying at the school, Matthew was going home to Stoke-on-Trent, and I took the train to Edinburgh. I had pictured spending the days with Lily much as we used to—shopping, doing the housework, enjoying the occasional outing—but I soon realised how foolish these imaginings were. Violet seldom left us alone for a moment, and she bossed Lily endlessly: clean this, cook that. Worst of all, though, were her comments about David. Once when Lily was reminiscing about his habit of putting out delicacies for the birds at Christmas, she exclaimed, "Heavens, Lily, what a feckless man, giving plum pudding to the sparrows. If it weren't for me, you wouldn't even have a roof over your head." Only Lily's quick glance prevented me from vehement contradiction.

To escape Violet's tyranny, I began to take the bus into the centre of Edinburgh, where I could wander around the museum or sit in a tearoom, reading a book. One afternoon I ended up in George Street, and the next thing I knew I was searching for Mr. Rosenblum's shop. Dusk was falling, it was close to four, and I was on the point of giving up when, on the other side of the street, I spotted the name. Slowly, almost on tiptoe, I crossed over. The other shops were brightly lit, even though there still wasn't much to buy. Mr. Rosenblum's, however, was dark, and when I put my face to the grimy window the display cases were empty. I searched in vain for the words FIFTH COLUMNIST scrawled there not so long ago. If anyone had asked, I would have said I had already given up all hope of Samuel; yet, staring at the desolate shop, I felt a painful rending as if, quite unbeknownst to myself, some tiny, hardy shoot of expectation had persisted and was only now, finally, being uprooted. As I sat on the bus back to Violet's, I counted off on my gloved fingers the days until I returned to the school. Mrs. Thornton's wish for me—that I would grow fond of the valley—was coming true.

I had been back at Glenaird for a little over a week when one evening a timid knock at the sitting room door interrupted my letter to Lily. I went to answer, expecting Mrs. Plishka; sometimes after supper I joined her and her husband in a hand of cards. Instead, a small boy swayed on the threshold.

"I know this isn't when you see people," Scott whispered. "I just feel so rotten."

In the surgery he began to cry. When his sobs tapered, I took his temperature. The mercury rose swiftly past a hundred. He told me that he ached all over, could hardly climb a flight of stairs, utter a sentence. I put him to bed in a private room and telephoned his housemaster.

"I thought he'd been shirking," growled the master. "He tried to get out of soccer yesterday."

"He has a temperature of a hundred and one," I said in my best official voice. "I'll let you know what the doctor says tomorrow."

I went back to my letter to Lily.

> *Maybe in the summer the two of us could take a holiday. A fortnight at the seaside. I'm sure by then hotels will be open again. We can stay somewhere posh and be waited on hand and foot. Weeks pass here without my spending a shilling. I'll have plenty saved by July.*

On my way to bed I stopped to check on Scott. He was asleep, but his hair was wet with perspiration and his breath rose in sour gusts. Watching him, I was suddenly afraid. It was one thing to have a patient ill in hospital, quite another here in this remote valley with no sister to turn to, no doctors on call. I telephoned Dr. Singer.

"Flu," he said, when I described the symptoms. "Diphtheria," as I continued.

Half an hour later we were standing on either side of Scott's bed. Together we ministered to the semiconscious boy. Dr. Singer listened to his chest, peered into his eyes. "I don't know what to think," he said at last, and promised to return first thing in the morning. After he had gone, I fetched a blanket and settled myself in an armchair near the door of the small room.

By morning Scott's temperature was 104. But when Dr. Singer

examined him, his skin was unblemished, his glands unswollen. The doctor took samples of urine and blood. Presently he telephoned to say that, according to the tests, Scott was in perfect health. "I'm baffled, Eva. Maybe this is just a bad case of flu?"

"Maybe," I said, but instinct told me otherwise.

During the days that followed I scarcely saw my flat. I was either in Scott's room or tending other patients. Dr. Singer called morning and evening, and Scott's friend, Fox, came steadfastly to ask after him. Besides them, my only company was the Plishkas. Anne and I sent notes but did not meet. I was worried, mostly on her behalf, a little on my own, that Scott's mysterious illness might prove contagious. Like most of the masters, she and Paul had no telephone.

One night when Scott was especially restless, I came back from fetching a basin of water to find the woman at the foot of his bed. She was leaning forward, watching him intently. Scott uttered a series of groans, the more heartrending for being almost inaudible. "Can't you make him better?" I begged. "He's only a child."

For a moment I thought she would shake me. "Eva, I can't save lives any more than you can. In fact less—I don't have your nursing skills. People can die at any age. One of my own children nearly died." Her eyes shone with sorrow.

Over the next few hours Scott's temperature slowly fell, and by morning he was sleeping quietly. After breakfast the other boys on the ward settled to homework, and I took advantage of the lull to have a bath. Waiting for the water to run hot, I caught sight of my reflection in the mirror. I wiped away the condensation to discover a half-familiar face. When had my cheekbones become so sharp, my eyes so large? Briefly I thought of the patients on the unit, the ones I felt sorriest for, who had lost their eyelids and were reduced to endless, ragged staring. Now I too looked more like a patient than a nurse. Don't be daft, I told myself. I had scarcely slept for a fortnight. No surprise if I was exhausted.

Later that morning—it must have been a Saturday—Matthew came to invite me to lunch. "Mrs. Plishka will watch Scott," he said. "I already asked her."

Although the sky was overcast, we decided to walk across the river to the village; I was desperate for fresh air. We strode along, our paces nicely matched, and Matthew pointed out the pheasants rooting in the frozen stubble, the bullfinches pecking at last summer's shrivelled rose hips. In the pub we sat near the fire, eating bangers and mash, while a father and son played darts by the bar. As I watched the father rocking back and forth, preparing to throw, I felt as I had sometimes in Glasgow after weeks of night duty, a stranger in the daylight world. Fortunately, Matthew seemed to understand and kept up an easy flow of undemanding conversation: teaching Milton, his ongoing struggles with Best.

When we emerged from the pub, the sun had broken through and the weathercock was glinting on the church steeple. Suddenly the idea came to me—I wondered why I hadn't thought of it before—that my grandparents might be buried here. I asked Matthew if we could take a look in the churchyard. As we pushed open the gate, half a dozen sheep surveyed us warily from among the gravestones. Matthew explained that the minister had died the previous spring and they had yet to appoint a new one. "A local farmer minds the place in exchange for grazing. What were your grandparents' names?"

"Malcolm. William and Morag Malcolm."

He began to examine the graves along the path. A ram rose from beside a fallen cross. I was watching it make its way between the stones when I caught sight of the girl. She raised a finger to her lips and beckoned. With a hasty glance at Matthew—he was peering at an inscription—I followed her between the graves to a tall yew tree on the south wall.

"Here they are," she said, gesturing towards two stones, leaning on a third. Close up I could see that her face was pinched with cold; she wore neither gloves nor scarf. Before I could urge her to dress more warmly, she scrambled over the wall.

I stared at the matching grey stones. Then I saw that the third gravestone, where the girl had stood, was for Barbara's sister, Elizabeth, the one who had died of polio, whose grave she had visited as a little girl. SUMMONED BY OUR SAVIOUR read the inscription. Beneath it was a knot of flowers. Quickly I stepped forward to press my lips to Elizabeth's stone.

"Your ancestors," said Matthew, when I showed him. "Maybe in the spring, after they've moved the sheep, we could plant flowers here—peonies or lavender—that will bloom year after year."

He was smiling at me, and after a moment I returned his smile. "I'd like that," I said.

Back at the san I hurried upstairs, worried Scott might have taken a turn for the worse, but as I reached his room the gentle percussion of Mrs. Plishka's knitting reassured me. She furled her needles with a smile. "He's getting better," she said.

Drawing near the bed, I saw she was right. Scott's breathing was easier and his cheeks were tinged with colour. After years of nursing I knew how easily a patient can slip back and forth across the line between health and illness, but I could not help hoping that he was at last on the mend.

That night, as I sat reading beside him, the woman again appeared at the foot of his bed. Since my arrival at Glenaird her occasional fierceness had been held in abeyance. Now it was as if the window had been abruptly thrown open onto the winter's night. A cold, crackling current swept through the room. "He's not yours," she said. "You need one of your own."

"What do you mean?"

"Remember David's wish. What do you need for happiness?"

She bent over me, and I understood her words. In my loneliness, I had been pretending Scott was my son and that these weeks of intimacy need have no end. "A family," I said.

She seemed to soften slightly. "Ask Matthew to plant heart's-ease on the graves. It was your grandmother's favourite flower."

"I will."

For some reason my acquiescence served only to exasperate her again. "Eva, use your brain. You're fond of Matthew, aren't you?"

I nodded. Fond was exactly the word. However often I counted his many virtues, there was none of that quickening of the eyes and limbs I had known with Samuel.

"Well, there you are." She drifted over to the bed. "Sleep," she whispered. "Sleep and grow strong."

Now that Scott was better, Dr. Singer said it was safe to see Anne again. During the intervening weeks her belly had grown, and she was convinced the baby was a boy. We headed along the road, bypassing the Grange, to the top of the track called Patten's First. The field below us was occupied by a flock of sheep, many of them ewes newly brought to lamb, and as we leaned on the gate, the back and forth of their bleating filled the air. I felt as if the world had been made afresh. Scott's recovery, Anne's baby, the brightness of the day, all were cause for rejoicing. "What a beautiful morning," I said.

"Yes. Paul's taking the boys on a run this afternoon."

I saw her smile as she said her husband's name, and I thought of how they were together. A continual flow of small gestures: hands meeting over a cup, a pat on the arm or shoulder. They were more than fond. "Have you chosen names?" I asked.

"Robert," Anne answered, without a second's hesitation.

A fortnight later I found a note on the san door—*4 a.m. gone to Perth Infirmary*—and presently Mr. Thornton telephoned with the news that Anne was safely delivered of a boy. The chapel bells pealed, and I joined the Plishkas in a toast. They served a curious colourless liquid which made me cough. "Very good," they said, as I tried to repeat their Polish.

Next day I was in the surgery, filling in the notes, when the girl appeared. Her stockings drooped and she was breathing hard. "Come for a walk," she said.

"I have to catch up on the notes. I've let them go for nearly a week."

"Please. There's a flock of geese I want to show you. They have beautiful long necks and dappled feathers."

She opened her eyes wide and I laid aside my pen. "All right. A very short walk."

We hurried downstairs and out into the damp afternoon. Rain threatened. Once more I was about to protest, but she took my arm. "The geese will be going home soon. Let's send a message to the snow princess."

As we reached Front Avenue, there came the sound of a car. The girl vanished behind a beech tree and Matthew's decrepit green Ford pulled up. We greeted each other and remarked on the wonderful news about the baby. "I'm on my way to Perth," he said. "Would you like a lift to see Anne?"

"But I don't have my things."

"What do you need? I can lend you money"—he delved into a pocket to demonstrate—"and a handkerchief. Clean, I promise."

His car, always noisy, had reached a new crescendo. As we clattered down the main road, he apologised for the muffler. I nodded, too excited for conversation. Because of the war I had never been assigned to the maternity ward and only once or twice had I seen a a newborn. At the door of Perth Infirmary, Matthew promised to be back in an hour. I watched him drive away and, turning to the hospital, forgot him. Inside, the familiar odour engulfed me. A couple of nurses were walking purposefully amid the uncertain visitors; I joined the latter.

Anne was sitting up in bed, her fair hair tied back, her face calm, and beside her, wrapped in a woolen blanket, still somewhat rumpled from his passage into the world, was Robert. Together we praised his eyelashes, his tiny fingers. I touched his cheek, dizzy with desire.

"Feel his hair," Anne instructed.

"Did everything go all right?" I asked.

"They told me . . . look, he's opening his eyes."

I leaned forward to catch my first glimpse of Robert's deep gaze.

On the drive back I could speak of nothing else. Matthew probably heard one word in ten, but he smiled and bobbed his head. We were almost back at the school, cresting the final rise, when he pulled over. "They claim babies can't really see," I was saying, "but I'm sure he was watching us."

He turned off the engine. In the sudden silence I heard the mournful cries of the lapwings watching over their nests in the nearby fields. Before I could ask what was wrong, Matthew was speaking.

"This isn't the way to ask," he said, "but will you marry me?"

I thought of Robert's tiny mauve hands, waving like sea anemones, his grey eyes. I looked over and saw how tightly Matthew held the steering wheel. In the fields the birds no longer sounded melancholy. Yes, yes, they seemed to cry; I had only to echo them. "Yes," I said.

"You will?" He sounded so incredulous that, at the same moment, we both burst out laughing. Awkwardly, across the gearshift and the brake, we embraced.

That evening Matthew came to my sitting room bearing a small box. He slid the ring, a sapphire with two diamonds, onto the appropriate finger. "The man in the shop said he could alter it, but there's no need, is there?"

"No, it's beautiful." I held out my hand for him to admire.

Neither of us knew what to say or do next. Then Matthew looked at the clock and announced he'd better be going. "Well, good night," he said, kissing my cheek. Touched by his ineptitude, I flung my arms around his neck and kissed him on the lips.

When his footsteps were gone, I sat down to wait. No one came. The chairs remained all four feet on the floor, the carpet lay flat, the pictures hung still. As the minutes passed, a kind of peace descended upon me.

I did not feel that I had to tell Matthew about the companions. Nor did I fear their intervention. From that day in the churchyard, when the girl had kept her distance, I knew they would not come between us. As for the other things, the fluttering of the heart, the eagerness to touch and hold, I looked down at the ring and thought perhaps such feelings could be learned. Perhaps we could learn them together.

14

Everyone was pleased by the news of our engagement. Mrs. Thornton took it as a personal triumph. "The first day I laid eyes on you," she said, "I told my husband you wouldn't last six months." Between us we agreed I would finish out the school year. Matthew and I would get married in the summer and in the autumn I would return as a master's wife. Anne burst into tears. So did Mrs. Plishka. Dr. Singer shook my hand and wished me joy. The girl brought a bunch of primroses. The woman exclaimed, *"C'est fantastique."*

The one person I did not tell was Lily. "I want to do it in person," I explained to Matthew and Anne. But it was more than that. A few days after his proposal I was stocking the medicine cupboard when I found myself remembering my conversation with Lily in the lane. Suddenly I wondered if she might still expect me to offer her a home. Of course, said Matthew over supper that night, and I could see he meant it. My own feelings, however, were more complicated; at the thought of living with both him and her, a kind of darkness came over me, as if upon reaching the climax of a book I turned to a blank page. Try as I might, I could not picture our household. On one pretext or another, I put off visiting Edinburgh until the Whitsun holiday in May. Then I wrote, asking if Lily could meet my train, hoping to speak to her alone, but she had a church meeting to attend.

As I climbed the gloomy stairs to Violet's flat, I repeated to myself the sort of remarks Daphne used to make. I was twenty-six, a grown woman; besides, Matthew had all the credentials of a good husband. Lily opened the door, dressed in her best suit. I was exclaiming how smart she looked when Violet appeared, resplendent in brown. "That coat's certainly seen better days," she said, kissing my cheek.

"Father gave it to me the winter I went to Glasgow." I turned to Lily. "Remember going to Forsythe's to choose it?"

"Thank goodness you got it before coupons."

I excused myself. After five years of rationing, Violet still had prewar soap, a privilege which, at Christmas, she had warned me not to abuse; now I took pleasure in lathering my hands vigorously. When I came into the kitchen, Lily was setting the table. "They must be overworking you at that school," she said. "Violet and I were both saying how pale you are."

"I'm fine." I was taken aback that she could not tell, just by my face, that something wonderful had happened. While Violet talked about the cleaning rota for the church, I crossed my legs and straightened my skirt. I had never worn a ring before and, to my eyes, the small stones were dazzling, but the aunts did not appear to notice. Violet continued to hold forth, with occasional comments from Lily. At last tea was served and I could wait no longer. "I've something to tell you," I said. "I'm engaged to one of the masters."

Violet bounded across the room. "Congratulations, my dear. May the Lord bring you many years of happiness. Oh, look at your ring. That's a sapphire, isn't it? Such a pretty stone."

Lily meanwhile sat as if nailed to her seat. I felt a despair which, now that the moment was here, seemed entirely predictable. When Violet, still exclaiming, had sat down again, Lily said quietly, "When did this happen?"

"A few weeks ago. I didn't want to tell you in a letter."

"How old is he?"

"Twenty-eight."

"How much money does he have?"

"Whatever he earns."

"Who's going to pay for the wedding?"

I had not thought of that. "I will," I said impulsively. "I have Father's money."

"That's not what he intended it for." She went over to the fire and rattled the poker in the grate until Violet complained she was wasting coal.

Not until after supper, when Violet went to turn down the beds, did I have a chance to speak to Lily alone. Then, desperate to placate her, I blurted out the invitation. "We thought you might come and live with us," I said. "Once we have a place of our own." She was at the sink and at first I thought she was going to continue to ignore me. She scrubbed furiously at a plate.

"Aunt Lily," I pleaded.

"The idea of you getting engaged to a total stranger, Eva. What on earth are you thinking of?"

"He's not a stranger to me."

"We know nothing about him. He could be the trunk murderer. Or Jack the Ripper." She set the plate to drain, started on another. "David's only been gone a few months. When I think how he was faithful to Barbara for a quarter of a century."

If she had hit me, I would not have been more confounded or more stricken. David was always in my thoughts, but it had never occurred to me that I was getting engaged within the traditional period of mourning; perhaps the years of nursing had dulled me to such distinctions.

By the time I left next morning, Lily had still not vouchsafed the smallest sign of approval. Staring out of the train window at the green blur of the newly planted fields, I thought she was right. During the war I had seen many short engagements, but now there was no need. We could wait another year; Matthew would understand. And surely Lily would come around when she got to know him and saw that we wanted to respect David's memory. As these sensible ideas took shape, my agitation was replaced by hunger. I had eaten almost no breakfast. I was unwrapping my sandwiches—meat paste and cucumber—when the door of the compartment slid open.

"Those look good." The woman took a seat opposite.

"What are you doing here?" I exclaimed. Although the companions could find me anywhere, I was startled that they would board a train.

She gave a little smile. "So how was Lily?" she said, gazing at me with her deep grey eyes so like those of Anne's small son.

"All right." Then I ended up telling her about Lily's reaction and how it seemed best to postpone the wedding. "I wouldn't mind being matron for another year."

The train lurched and we both seized an armrest. "Lily was just surprised," the woman said. "You were very closemouthed. And you know David wanted you to get married. Besides," she added, "it would be hard to change your mind now. Mr. Thornton has already advertised your job."

The engine let out a piercing whistle and we plunged into darkness. When the train emerged from the tunnel, I was once more facing an empty seat. The thought of someone else occupying my cosy rooms gave me a pang, but the woman's comment about David had comforted me. After all, Lily had said the same thing. And as for Lily herself, she had never liked change, but that didn't mean she wouldn't come around. I picked up a sandwich and began to eat.

In July I treated two sprained ankles at sports day; then my duties were over. Matthew was going home to Stoke-on-Trent, and I was staying in Edinburgh until the wedding. We had chosen a Saturday in August, almost the exact anniversary, Lily was swift to point out, of David's death. Besides the aunts, I knew no one in the city. Mrs. Nicholson had moved down to Bath, and I had lost touch with Shona and Flo. Matthew and I had booked the church and sent out invitations before he went south, but the flowers and reception were still to be organised. And I had no dress. For years Lily had kept Barbara's dress at the back of her wardrobe. Now it turned out to be too small; I couldn't even begin to do up the buttons. Lily, however, only sighed and went on scouring the knives. Meanwhile, Violet reminisced about her own nuptials but offered no practical assistance. I took to leaving the flat, on the pretext of errands, and going instead to the park at the end of the road.

One afternoon as I sat watching some boys play cricket, the woman strolled across the grass to join me. Her yellow cotton dress was very like one Lily had worn twenty years before. "What an excellent overarm that boy has," she said.

The boy in question had just bowled a thoroughly mediocre over. Now, following her gaze, I saw he was sending balls whizzing towards the wicket.

"You know," she said, "what always saved me from difficult situations were my friends. You have friends too."

"Not in Edinburgh."

"It's not hard to get here. Oh, good hit!"

The ball was still soaring as she rose to her feet and headed towards the gate. When the next over began, the bowler had returned to his former mediocrity.

Back at the flat, I wrote to Daphne and, once the letter was posted, felt more cheerful than I had in weeks. After supper, I suggested a round of whist. Lily dealt and Violet campaigned to raise the stakes from a farthing to a penny. In bed, however, the jolliness of the game vanished. I lay there, puzzling over the companions' role in my upcoming marriage. One evening towards the end of term when we were strolling across the cricket pitch, Matthew had confided in me his version of the day we got engaged. "I felt as if I were hypnotised," he said. "After I dropped you off at the infirmary,

I was on my way to the bookshop. Suddenly I found myself stopping in front of a jeweller's." He laughed. "Once I'd bought the ring, there seemed no point in delaying so I proposed on the drive home."

In the shadow of the cricket pavilion he drew me to him. Since our first clumsy embrace, he had grown more ardent and I had felt my own stirrings. But that evening, after a couple of kisses, I had said I must get back to my patients.

I shifted uneasily. Beneath me the bed creaked. It was not only Matthew whose actions were governed. Hadn't the girl arranged for me to be walking up Front Avenue as he drove by? Anxiety seized me. I remembered how the companions had helped me to a job at Mr. Laing's and then got me fired; how after bringing me together with Samuel, they had torn us apart. Now they could not do enough to make sure I married Matthew, but who knew what their motives were or when they might change their minds? Once again I was struck by the notion that all the seemingly random events of my life were in fact organised according to some hidden pattern I knew nothing about.

"I won't betray you," I whispered. "Don't betray me."

As so often before, Daphne came to my rescue. During several day trips from Glasgow she found a dressmaker, booked a hotel for the reception, ordered the flowers. And, like the woman, she reassured me about Lily. "She's just scared of losing you," she said. "She'll come round." Even as the day drew near, this seemed to be happening: Lily began to take an interest in my plans, make the odd matrimonial joke. On the morning of the wedding she stood behind me doing up the thirty hooks on the back of my dress. "There. Let me have a look at you."

When I turned around she stared, without saying a word, until I tugged at the bodice. "Is it all right?"

"I was just thinking how much you look like Barbara. She was a lovely bride." She kissed me and hurried away to help Violet.

Alone, I approached the mirror. There stood a young woman in a high-necked full-skirted dress. My trunks were packed and I was ready to embark upon what the chaplain called the journey of matrimony. Then I thought of Lily's comment. Barbara, too, must have stood before a mirror on her wedding day, imagining a life bright with promise.

The door opened. "What are you doing?" Violet demanded. "Don't you know it's bad luck for a bride to see her reflection?"

She stepped in front of the mirror, immense in her beige frock, and I smelled her dry gardenia perfume. "The time to look in a mirror," she went on, "is after the wedding, with your husband. It brings good luck. Andrew and I did that, and we were happy for thirty-seven years. God rest his soul."

I had not laid eyes on Matthew for nearly five weeks, and as I walked up the aisle on Mr. Thornton's arm and saw him, waiting at the altar, I was amazed at how handsome he was. For months I had been rolling back my ambivalence. Now, as the minister joined us together, it finally tumbled away. How gladly I gave and received the promises of marriage. We turned to face our guests. In the front pew, Lily, Violet, and Matthew's parents stood watery-eyed. For a moment, all I could think of was David. Then the organ started, Matthew gave me a gentle tug, and we were walking down the aisle, past other friends from the infirmary and the school. And there, standing near the back, were the companions, dressed in their best clothes, smiling.

15

Marriage, it turned out, did not entirely banish memories of Samuel. I meant to forget him, I had the best of intentions, but in the long hours of housework and reading he sometimes slipped into my mind, and before I knew it I was picturing him as he bent over a patient or leaned towards the cinema screen. Sometimes, I'm ashamed to say, this happened even when Matthew and I were together, listening to the wireless or playing cribbage; happily, he never seemed to notice.

And then all thoughts of Samuel vanished. I was pregnant. I knew, with utter certainty, after only a few weeks but until Dr. Singer confirmed my condition, I mentioned it to no one. During this period of secrecy, I oscillated between joy and dread. I could not help worrying that history would prevail: the life growing within me would cost my own. Then I would remind myself that

Anne had confessed to similar premonitions, and here she was, fit and well, with Robert.

The companions seemed to guess my state almost as soon as I did myself. Because no house was available in the school grounds, Matthew had rented a cottage on a small farm a mile west of Glenaird, and there was always fetching and carrying to be done. One morning as I stepped out to the clothesline, the woman barred my way. "You have to be careful now," she said, taking the laundry basket out of my hands. Between them, she and the girl hung the wet sheets on the line.

The day after my appointment with Dr. Singer, I broke the news to Matthew at breakfast. "How could you be?" he said. His hand jerked and the boiled egg I had just set before him flew to the floor. On the one occasion before our wedding when we'd discussed children, Matthew had claimed he was too young for fatherhood. "You're twenty-eight," I had said. "The prime of life." I had not thought he was serious.

Now the viscous mess of egg on the linoleum made my stomach heave, and the reflection of the single bulb above the table off Matthew's glasses hid his expression. Before I could overcome my queasiness, he glanced at his watch, announced he was late for morning prayers, and hurried from the room. A moment later came the cranking of the car. As the engine fired, I rushed to the door. Too late. All that remained was a plume of exhaust hanging in the chilly air.

I wandered out to the main road. The hills were hidden in mist, and the narrow strip of wet macadam stretched to the horizon with neither car nor tractor in sight. I was standing, staring bleakly in the direction of the school, when the woman tapped my shoulder.

"Come inside," she said. "It's freezing." Her silvery hair was beaded with moisture.

She led the way indoors, and there, to my amazement, a middle-aged man was seated on our sofa. He had the ruddy cheeks of a countryman and the same kind of moustache as David had favoured. I sat down in the armchair, studying him as closely as I dared. He looked familiar, but for the life of me I could not place him. The infirmary had filled my head with faces briefly glimpsed.

"That's better," said the woman. "You shouldn't be loitering in the cold."

"My father had a theory about the weather," the man said in a soft Highland accent. "Buchan's cold spells. It all has to do with certain key days—you know, if December the sixth is warm then the rest of the month will be cold."

"That sounds like mumbo jumbo," said the woman.

"No, no, it was quite scientific, but we're not here to prattle about the climate." A smile creased his cheeks. "Don't mind Matthew. He behaved badly this morning, but he'll come round. Men are odd about these matters. I myself was quite shocked to learn that my dear wife was expecting."

The woman nodded. "You must take care of yourself. Eat sensibly and don't worry. When I was carrying my first child, my mother made me eat an apple and an orange every day."

She dispatched me to put on the kettle, and when I returned the room was empty. Still in a daze, I finished stoking the fires and made soup. Only as I sat down to write to Lily did I realise who the man reminded me of: Barbara's uncle Jack. His wedding photograph had stood, next to that of her parents, on the sideboard at Ballintyre.

Did Lily still have it? I wondered. And why, after all these years, was a new companion visiting? Then the excitement of telling Lily about the baby dispelled even these speculations.

An hour later I heard the latch lift. Before I could rise, Matthew had me in his arms. "Eva, I'm sorry I was such a beast." He kissed me, took off his glasses, and kissed me again.

"So you don't mind?" I whispered.

"On the contrary, I'm delighted. I was just taken aback. I thought being a father was one of those impossible things, the sort the White Queen tells you to practise imagining before breakfast."

The difficult hours vanished like ice on the griddle. That evening over supper we discussed names. He favoured the heroic: Frederick, Tristram, Georgiana. I was more inclined to the biblical: Mary, Sarah, Ruth.

"Do you want a boy or a girl?" I asked.

Matthew wrinkled his forehead. "Both—either—I don't care."

"Nor do I." But I was sure I carried a daughter. For the first and only time I could read the future.

A few weeks later, walking along the main road to visit Anne, I saw a boy approaching. Head lowered, he was dawdling along, swishing idly at the long grass on the verge with a stick, the picture of dejection. I must have walked like that, I thought, as day after day I wandered home from school with only the girl for company. Then, at the same instant, Scott and I recognised each other. He dropped the stick and ran towards me.

"Matron!"

We shook hands. In the months since I'd seen him he had grown several inches, and everything about him was too long and thin. I started walking again and he fell in beside me. "This is the wrong direction for you," I said.

"It doesn't matter. I haven't seen you for ages."

"We live out at a farm now. You know I got married."

"The new matron is awful. She doesn't allow any visitors."

Other people had made similar remarks about my successor, a London woman who'd rejected all my overtures of friendship; I tried not to show my pleasure at Scott's comment. Instead I asked interested questions about his schoolwork. When we reached Anne's house, he gazed at me beseechingly until I invited him to tea next day.

Inside, Robert was asleep and Anne was at the kitchen table, peeling brussels sprouts. I made tea and told her about meeting Scott. "All the time he was ill, I thought if I could nurse him back to health, he would live happily ever after. And there he was, the picture of misery."

Anne plucked at a sprout. "It's awful being a child. I remember wanting things so badly and feeling so powerless."

"What did you want?"

"Piano lessons. More attention from my father. To be taller than Oliver." She cut a cross in the bottom of a sprout. "What about you?"

I gazed around Anne's cosy kitchen, the kettle still steaming on the stove, the gingham curtains hanging in the windows. "To be like everyone else," I said. It seemed a safe approximation. "Yet here we are having babies."

"It'll be different for them, though, won't it? They can have piano lessons if they like."

I did not dare to answer. Anne peeled another couple of sprouts. "Of course, our parents said that too. Sometimes I watch Robert sleeping. One minute he's perfectly peaceful, and the next it's as if a storm has struck."

"Perhaps he has bad dreams," I offered.

"But how does he know about anything bad? Paul and I dote on him, yet already we can't protect him. There's something in the air"—she spread her hands—"a dark wind that blows him dark thoughts."

I sympathised with Anne's anxieties but they were the anxieties of plenty; how happy I would be when I could worry about my plump, healthy baby having bad dreams. For now, all my wishes, all the good luck I had garnered from magpies and black cats, ladders and four-leaf clovers, was bent on that single moment of double desire: to bring my daughter safely into the world and to remain here to show it to her.

The next day when I told Scott about the baby, he smiled and said he had always wanted a brother or sister. "My friend Fox has two younger sisters. I helped one of them learn to read. And in Nigeria my father's assistant had a baby, but I wasn't allowed to play with him. They said he was an *abiku*."

"*Abiku?*"

"May I have some more toast? A baby who's taken over by a spirit." He began to spread the jam. "People recognise them when they leave their cribs before they can walk. *Abiku* don't live long, because the spirits only want to visit the world for a while. Then they get tired and want to go home. Are you coming to the carol service? I have a solo, an awfully small one."

"Goodness," I murmured, remembering the Jewish folk tale Samuel had told me. Then I saw Scott's puzzled face and quickly assured him I would be at the service. What were his plans for Christmas? He was still talking about going to stay with Fox, their hopes for snow, when Matthew arrived home.

"Come again," I said, as Scott put on his bicycle clips.

"But not tomorrow," added Matthew. "We'll be in Perth."

We stood in the doorway, waving, as he rode unsteadily away. "I didn't know we were going to Perth," I said.

"Well, I had to say something to stop him coming every day."

As we made Welsh rabbit, Matthew told me that Mr. Thornton had promised us a school house by the end of June. "I wish it could be next week. I worry about you here alone."

I looked up from the cheese grater, touched by the sudden intimation of his concern. I had often thought that, between the time he drove away in the morning and returned at night, Matthew forgot me utterly.

Scott got his wish for snow with a vengeance. The winter of '46–'47 was the worst in fifty years. By January our windows were lined with ice and even the pigs at the farm were subdued. The journey to the school could only be made on foot. Twice our electricity failed, and once the pipes froze. One day when Matthew was teaching and I had climbed into bed to keep warm, the woman appeared. "For heaven's sake," she exclaimed. "You don't have the brains you were born with. What about Anne's spare room?"

The next morning, in icy sunshine, Matthew tied our suitcases to a sledge and we set off along the main road. No tractors or ploughs had passed and we had only his steps from other journeys to guide us. On the far side of the valley the hills shone so brightly my eyes ached. Matthew compared us to Scott and Oates and, when I protested, substituted Amundsen.

We stayed with Anne and Paul for nearly a month, an oddly happy period. Anne and I cooked and played with Robert. Matthew and Paul stoked the fires and fetched groceries. In the evenings the four of us settled to canasta and gin rummy. My only real concern was Lily; for a fortnight there was no mail. Then a letter arrived. They had abandoned their top-floor flat for that of the widower downstairs, who had a boy to help with the heavy work. "Violet has grown positively lax," she wrote, "and we have a hand of whist after supper." She and I were both sorry, I think, when the thaw took us back to our respective homes.

Soon after midsummer the new house became available. I was eight months pregnant, a ship in full sail, and although both Anne and Lily had offered to help with the move, neither was available. Robert had measles, and the day before Lily was due to arrive, she sent a letter. "Violet has hurt her wrist and insists it's broken. The doctor thinks she might have a sprain."

Since her reaction to my engagement, I had felt myself estranged from Lily. Now the sharpness of my disappointment made me re-alise that my coldness was as superficial as a layer of dust; beneath it lay all my love for her, unchanged. "Isn't there something we can do?" I asked Matthew.

"We could send a telegram saying you've broken a leg."

In spite of myself, I smiled. "We'd better keep our excuses for after the baby. Then we can all three claim broken legs."

On the day of the move, Matthew forbade me to lift so much as a book. "It's your job to supervise. Point your hand and say, 'Take the wardrobe in there, my men.'"

For our wedding, his parents had given us several pieces of Victorian furniture: a wardrobe, a sideboard, a rolltop desk, a table, a wing-back chair. Now these were fetched from storage and installed in the new house, along with the furnishings from the cottage.

"Where do you think the desk should go?" Matthew said. We were standing in the living room. Through the open door we could hear the men swearing as they manoeuvred it down the corridor.

"How about that corner?" I suggested.

"Wouldn't it be better under the window? There's more light."

"Fine."

"You're sure?" He patted my shoulder. "We won't be able to move this furniture once a week." At the cottage in the steading, I had rearranged our small number of possessions so often it had become a joke.

As soon as the men were through the door, I excused myself and went to the baby's room. This side of the house faced the main road, though the road itself was hidden by a copse of firs. Gazing out of the window, I saw, in the topmost branches, a group of black birds, cawing and swaying.

"What are those?" I asked when Matthew came in.

"Rooks. You can tell because they're in a crowd. Rooks live in a rookery, whereas crows are solitary. What about the chest of drawers?"

That night in our new bedroom I could not sleep. I lay on my back, my belly pressing down, missing the noises of the animals at the farm. On the far side of the room I saw the dark outline of the new wardrobe. Suddenly there was a soft thud and, after a brief interval, another. I crept out of bed and along the corridor. The sounds came from the living room. As my hand reached the doorknob, I heard something clatter to the floor.

There were no curtains at the windows, and the room was silvery with moonlight. I entered in time to see the wing-back chair rise unsteadily. The desk twitched and a lamp floated above the wireless. For five minutes gentle pandemonium reigned. Then the spirits returned each piece of furniture to its exact and proper place. I went back to bed and slept soundly.

At breakfast I told Matthew I must finish unpacking; the baby might come at any moment. But I was too distracted to work steadily. I would open a box of china and, after unwrapping a plate or two, wander over to a suitcase. As I hung up a blouse, it would occur to me that it was time for a cup of tea. A fortnight later, when Anne was out of quarantine, she found me still surrounded by boxes; only the baby's room was ready. At the sight of the chaos, she handed me Robert. "Let's start in the kitchen," she said. "Show me where you want things."

By the end of the afternoon, most of the boxes were empty and Anne had promised to return the next day. Alone, I decided to go and pick raspberries. The girl had recommended a place at the back of the Grange where the canes grew wild. Earlier I had heard the ratcheting of the mower, and now, as I walked across the lawn behind the big house, the soft green smell rose around me, mingling with the gnats.

Fanning away the insects, I caught sight of my belly, strange yet familiar in its largeness. Beneath my palm the baby moved. Such a specific feeling, both part of me and apart. A foot or elbow jutted out, and it came to me that, just as my baby pressed against me, so had I once pressed against Barbara. She too had felt the drumming of my heels against the thin skin of her belly, swimming towards daybreak. I used to think she had never known me. On the contrary, she had known me intimately.

That night when we sat down to supper, Matthew raised his glass. "A toast," he said, "to our new home, Rookery Nook. May health and happiness dwell at our hearth."

"To Rookery Nook." I sipped cautiously from my own glass; these days even the smallest amount of beer made me dizzy.

As we ate, Matthew told me how he had come home from school to see the rooks dive-bombing the treetops. "They were trying to chase away an owl. There must be some chicks left in the nests."

"And did the owl leave?" I asked and, before he could answer, began to yawn helplessly. Suddenly, sitting at the table even a minute longer was impossible. Although the sun was still shining and would be for several hours, I headed for bed. Between the cool sheets sleep claimed me instantly.

I woke in darkness, bewildered. For a brief moment I thought I was at Ballintyre, the branches of the apple tree scratching at my window, Lily and David sleeping nearby. Then I came back to myself in this bed, with my husband, and I knew what had roused me. I went to the toilet and then woke Matthew.

He sat up, wide-eyed and anxious in his striped pyjamas. "Should we go to the hospital?" he asked.

"Not yet. I need to move around."

Together in our nightclothes we walked up and down the main road. The longest day of the year was only a few weeks past; already the sky was lightening. From the trees came the sounds of birds beginning to stir, and in the fields I could distinguish the gleam of newly shorn sheep.

Arm in arm we strolled back and forth. No one else was awake and it was as if the world that emerged from darkness appeared solely for our benefit. As a boy Matthew had memorised a poem a week. At my request, he rolled out the cadences of "Tintern Abbey."

> "And I have felt
> A presence that disturbs me with the joy
> Of elevated thoughts; a sense sublime
> Of something far more deeply interfused,
> Whose dwelling is the light of setting suns,
> And the round ocean and the living air,
> And the blue sky, and in the mind of man."

Soon the sun rose over the hills, and the tall grass along the roadside was bright with dew. More and more frequently I stopped to catch my breath and count. Shouldn't we go? Matthew would ask, and I would beg another poem. At six we went inside to dress and collect the suitcase that had stood at the foot of the bed since we moved. I wouldn't let Matthew drive faster than twenty mph for fear I might cry out and startle him. We were at the infirmary by seven. A brisk staff nurse dispatched him to the waiting room. "We'll call you when there's news, sir."

Now all the names I had learned from textbooks were amplified into new meaning. And all the words I had offered in consolation to patients in pain evaporated. From somewhere nearby I heard a series of piercing screams, and in the interval before the next contraction, I experienced pity for this other sufferer. Then, as the nurse said, "Hush, hush," I realised it was I who had screamed. Another spasm rushed through me and I screamed again. The magical summer night, the beauty of the morning, vanished. I had never known anything but pain.

At last the baby began to move, to move in response to my movements. The pain changed. I had never felt so alive. Around me I saw the brightly lit figures of the nurses and the doctor, urging me on. And I went on.

Everything converged into that time and place as you came into the world.

Part IV

YOU

16

After six days at the infirmary Matthew brought us home. You spent the journey open-eyed and silent as I pointed out landmarks. "There's Huntingtower Castle, Ruth. . . . Here's where Matthew proposed." The moment I laid eyes upon you, I had known your name with the same immediate conviction as David had known mine. As we pulled up outside the house, I was struck by the amazing fact: only two of us had left, three of us were returning.

Mrs. Plishka rushed out, waving her apron. "Eva, Matron McEwen, Mrs. Livingstone," she exclaimed.

"This is Ruth."

"Darling," said Mrs. Plishka, and poured out a torrent of Polish.

Matthew had hired her to help for a month. Beforehand I had protested the extravagance; now I was glad to have those days to devote to you. The weather was unusually fine, and while Matthew and Paul played golf, I spent many hours with Anne in the garden. Her mother had managed to get hold of a copy of Dr. Spock's book about babies, and we took turns reading it aloud. Or Anne weeded with Robert and I sat with you in a deck chair beneath the laburnum tree. The blossoms spun a cocoon of golden shade, like the willow tree in Troon, and I remembered the endless afternoons I had passed there, plotting heroic futures, while David fished nearby. Then I would think of Lily. I longed for her to meet you, but Violet insisted she could not manage alone, even for a weekend.

There was no delay, however, in introducing you to the companions. On our second day back, as soon as Matthew left to fetch Mrs. Plishka, they appeared. I was at the sink, rinsing a cup, when I heard the woman say, "Eva, we came to meet Ruth."

She stood in the kitchen doorway wearing the same yellow dress as at the cricket match; behind her stood the girl, hands clasped. "We came to meet Ruth," she repeated. "I know it's awkward but we couldn't wait."

Both her use of my name and her apology were unusual, but in my excitement I barely noticed. I led the way to your crib and lifted the blanket so that they could see you sleeping, your arms and legs still coiled in the embrace of the womb. You had the frowning, elderly expression of very young babies, as if you had recently arrived from another world and found this one sadly wanting.

"She looks like a little Buddha," said the girl.

"Buddha," said the woman. "She's exquisite. How dark her hair is—and see, her ears are like shells. Hello, Ruth." She bent to kiss your cheek and I remembered she too had had children, and not just children but a child who nearly died. As she straightened, I saw her eyes bright with unshed tears.

For a fortnight after our return, the only sounds at night were your cries and those of the owls hunting in the woods. Then I woke one night to hear the scrapes and thuds. My heart leapt in panic. What if the spirits, not knowing their strength, made you fly across the room? Or dropped something on the cot? I raced out of bed.

On the threshold a low sweet humming stopped me. By the light from the hall I saw the cot sway. They were holding it just above the floor, rocking it gently, so that you might sleep with greater ease.

Finally, after many letters and negotiations, Lily arranged to come for a fortnight at the end of September. Although she had persuaded a distant cousin to stay with Violet, I was on tenterhooks that something might go wrong at the last moment. While Matthew went to Perth to meet her, I waited anxiously, plumping the pillows on the sofa, moving the knickknacks around the mantelpiece. At last came the noise of a car rattling over the gravel. I flew out of the house. Matthew was approaching, a suitcase in either hand. And there was Lily, standing beside the car in her white blouse and dark skirt. I ran into her arms.

As I felt her cheek warm against my own and breathed in her familiar talcum powder, my adult life dropped away. All the years of childhood and youth, when she had been my main refuge, returned. "Aunt Lily," I stammered.

Presently we stepped apart. Matthew had disappeared into the house, and save for the car, still creaking from the journey, and a single rook cawing in the treetops, everything was quiet.

"Oh, Eva," she said, "you don't know how I've missed the countryside."

In spite of my protests, Lily cleaned the house from end to end, polishing floors and windows and fireplaces until they shone. Together we rearranged the furniture, although the desk, which I would have liked to move into a corner of the living room, was beyond us. When she was not cleaning or cooking, Lily took you for walks in the pram I had inherited from Anne. In the evenings she embroidered your christening robe. Whatever small difficulties still lingered from the time of my engagement vanished. She liked Matthew—and you, she adored. As I watched her singing "Oh, my darling Clementine" and telling you stories about Rapunzel and the Little Mermaid, I thought how she had given up her life to care for me and gone on to lose, at a blow, her home and her place in the world. How could my marriage not have struck her as yet another kind of loss? Only now, as she held you in her arms, could she believe there was gain too.

One chilly afternoon, when the leaves blew in handfuls of red and gold across the road, I asked Matthew to drive us around the valley to the village; I wanted to show Lily the Malcolms' graves. You fretted until the first cottages came into view, then fell asleep. I tucked you into the passenger seat and, leaving Matthew to keep watch, led Lily to the churchyard. As we passed the school, I glimpsed the rows of children at their desks and recounted my previous visit.

"But what made you think they were her initials?" said Lily. "Plenty of people must have them."

I stared at the ground, momentarily silenced. Why did you throw the stone? Catherine asked. Who taught you cat's cradle? Shona said. "Somehow I was certain," I offered at last.

The sheep had gone, and the gate to the churchyard stood ajar. I led the way to the yew tree. The previous autumn Matthew had planted lavender and heart's-ease on the graves. I knelt to pluck the dead flowers.

"What a beautiful situation," said Lily. "Did I tell you that Mrs. Wright organised the church fete committee to take care of David's and Barbara's graves?"

Next summer, I thought, next summer I would take you there, and Matthew too. "Oh, I am glad," I said. "And here's Elizabeth. Barbara's older sister."

"Gracious me." Lily stepped forward to examine the stone. "She must be the girl in the photograph."

"What photograph?" From where I knelt, my hands full of faded blossoms, I could not see her face, nor she mine.

"When I finally sorted out David's papers, there was a snapshot of Mr. and Mrs. Malcolm with a girl who wasn't Barbara."

Before I could question her further, Matthew was calling my name. Lily said she would take a quick look at the church, and I hurried back to the car. You lay where I had left you on the seat, wailing, while Matthew hovered over you, wringing his hands. "Thank goodness," he said. "I haven't a clue what she wants."

Muttering about cigarettes, he headed to the pub, and I rocked you into silence. Although Matthew doted on you, he was hopeless at fatherhood. Anne, and even Lily, joked about his clumsiness, but I was not bothered. David had grown close to me only when I began to walk and talk; Matthew would be the same. Meanwhile, I was happy to have you to myself. Sometimes I felt almost guilty at the degree to which you had replaced him. When he talked about partition in India, much in the news at that time, or his classes, I would nod as if listening, but really my mind was filled with your crystalline eyes and dimpled limbs.

The second Sunday of Lily's visit, we had your christening. After the boys filed out of chapel, the minister led the remainder of the congregation to the font. Lily, Anne, and Mrs. Thornton were to be the godparents. As I took my place beside Matthew, I spotted the woman and the girl standing at the back, beside a pillar. They had dressed for the occasion, not as at my wedding but in sombre old-fashioned clothes, more funereal than festive. The woman wore a misshapen black hat, most unbecoming.

You followed the proceedings, silent and alert in Lily's arms, until the minister reached for you; then you uttered a single sharp cry. I raised my head and found the woman's eyes fixed upon me with an expression of urgent gravity. Immediately I thought of you. Now that you were here I had inherited all the anxieties Anne used to speak of. If you sneezed, was it pneumonia? If you cried, were you afraid of light? dark? the kettle? the rooks? I stared back at the woman, begging for a hint, and she stepped behind the pillar.

The minister gave the blessing and everyone crowded around with congratulations. Anne said how pretty Ruth Barbara Livingstone was. Mrs. Thornton claimed you had the hands of a musician. The classics master remarked that you were no heavier than a pint of beer. We adjourned for sherry at the Thorntons'.

As soon as we arrived back at Rookery Nook, Lily changed out of her good suit and began to bustle about with a dustpan and brush; she was leaving the next day and was determined that not the smallest speck of dust should survive her visit. Matthew announced he was going to dig the garden. I nursed you. As you nuzzled my breast, I recalled the woman's face. Some of my elation slipped away.

When you fell asleep, I persuaded Lily to stop her scrubbing and join me in a cup of tea. Settled in the wing-back chair, she remarked how different your christening had been from mine. "That was such a sad day. Well, how could it not be, the day after Barbara's funeral? The church was freezing, and no one was there except Violet, David, me, and Mr. Waugh. You let out a good yell when the water touched you, just like Ruth. Afterwards we put you to sleep in a drawer beside the stove. Barbara was so superstitious she hadn't even bought a cradle."

Absentmindedly Lily fingered an earring, one of the same gold rings she had used to let me slip in and out of her ears. "Do you remember," she said, "that time you climbed out of your crib and made your way to the top of the stairs?"

"How old was I?"

"A little older than Ruth, but only a month or two. I look at her and I'm amazed. She could no more leave her crib than pigs can fly. Yet there you were at the top of the stairs. I'm not sure even David believed me." Lily shook her head. "I'm not sure I believed myself."

Everything in the room rose slightly and rotated into a new position. *Abiku,* I thought; they were here even then. "Do you think," I said, "Barbara was fey?"

"Fey?"

"You know, like seeing things other people don't see, or—" I stopped, afraid of saying too much.

Lily's mouth opened in an *oh* of surprise. "I haven't thought of this in years. Once I came into the kitchen at Ballintyre, and Barbara was sitting at the table, topping and tailing gooseberries and chatting away. She was quite flustered to see me."

"Did you hear what she was saying?"

"I did at the time. I caught a couple of sentences but I've long since forgotten them. We all talk to ourselves, but I do remember thinking that Barbara really did seem to be addressing another person. For a moment I even wondered if she was hallucinating." She cocked her head. "Is that Ruth?"

It was Matthew, wanting my advice about perennials. As I followed him outside, a tremendous gaiety bubbled up. The companions were not merely sent by Barbara. They had visited her too. Maybe we even shared them.

"What is it?" asked Matthew. "Do you think larkspur are a mistake?"

"No, no," I said, "larkspur will be perfect."

17

Lily's thank-you letter was folded around a photograph the size of a playing card. The black-and-white had faded to sepia and one corner was ragged, as if chewed by a baby, or a dog, but there was no mistaking what lay within the camera's lens. From other pictures I recognised Barbara's parents, Mr. and Mrs. Malcolm, framed by the back door of the Grange. The third figure I recognised from my own life: standing between the Malcolms, squinting slightly in the sunlight, was the girl. The photograph weighed no more than a leaf, yet it was the key to a room which, for many years, I had been wanting to enter.

I must have made a noise, gasped or sighed. Across the table, Matthew looked up from the newspaper. "My grandparents," I said, offering the photograph. "And Barbara's older sister, Elizabeth."

He raised the picture to the light and glanced from it to me and back again. "She looks a little like you," he said, "the same dark eyebrows and high forehead. I think Ruth will have them too." He returned to his paper, leaving me to marvel, again, at how easy he was to deceive.

On the way to Anne's that afternoon the girl stepped out from between the beech trees. I stopped, holding tight to the pram. "Hello——" I was about to add "Elizabeth," but something in her face made me hesitate. I remembered in the churchyard how she had shielded the third grave from my view.

"I found some chestnuts." She held out her cupped hands. "For Ruth." She smiled up at me shyly, her cheeks rosy. In the middle of her high forehead was a smudge.

"I'll give them to her when she wakes." I smiled back and laid the chestnuts in a corner of the pram. There was no reason to break the habit of a lifetime.

The girl's identity seemed so overwhelmingly obvious—only a local child would know about the California redwood—that I wondered why I hadn't guessed it sooner. Several reasons came to mind. David and Lily, although they spoke often of Barbara, seldom mentioned her family. Then, too, the companions were so much alive that it was hard to connect them with the dead. The main reason for my obtuseness, however, I understood only later: they themselves had not wanted me to guess.

Naturally, after this revelation I speculated about the woman, and one day, when we were talking in the living room, I went so far as to ask whether she too was related to Barbara. She vanished, and half a dozen books clattered from the bookcase to the floor. But the next morning, as soon as Matthew drove away, she was back again. Gone were the companions' huffs and absences. Nowadays neither of them ever left us alone for long. They were in love with you, and no amount of bad behaviour on my part could keep them away.

At first I was thrilled by their affection; month by month, I grew less certain. When you were a baby, your days spent between food and sleep, their presence seemed to make little difference. Soon, though, you began to recognise and remember, your hands grasped greedily, you slept through the night and learned to crawl at a furious pace and, rather unsteadily, to walk. Matthew made jokes about the next Olympics and compared you with Francina Blankers-Koen, the Dutchwoman who had won four medals in London shortly before your first birthday. Then, when the companions appeared, I wanted to ask them to stay away. I could not wish upon you that solitude which they had brought me and which you, at last, had broken.

My desires, however, were irrelevant. You were the arbitrator. When you were a baby, I was sure I had seen your eyes follow their comings and goings, heard you coo in response to their questions. But once you learned to talk, you acknowledged them neither by speech nor gesture. Even when the girl played "Peek-a-boo," you paid no heed. Could you have lost the ability to see them, as an adult grows deaf to the squeak of the bat? Or had I been mistaken all along?

One rainy afternoon in the spring of your second year, I was at the ironing board when you called, "Mummy, come find me."

Obediently I set aside the iron. As soon as I opened the living room door, I saw you crouched between the pedestals of the desk; the companions were making a show of searching for you.

The woman went over to the sofa and peered behind it. "Ruth," she said, "where are you?"

You stayed quiet, motionless.

The girl looked behind the curtains, under the table. At last she tiptoed to the desk and squatted down a few feet away. You did not even glance in her direction. After a moment she tossed back her braids and retired to the sofa with the woman.

I approached the desk and you erupted in giggles. "Oh, there you are!" I scooped you into my arms.

Anne had remarked, on more than one occasion, that recovering from Robert's birth took longer than she expected, and for months I clung to this explanation. I'm still recovering, I would tell myself. That was why washing the dishes, sweeping the floor, making the bed took so much longer. But with each passing season it became harder to ignore that something was amiss. One day in the midst of laying the fire, I felt in my side an odd, deep pain, and as I knelt there I suddenly recognised it; it was a larger, fiercer version of the pain that had assailed me the afternoon I first saw the California red-wood. Perhaps I was ill, I thought. Perhaps I had been ill for several years.

Slowly I rolled the paper into knots and crisscrossed the kindling as Lily had taught me. It was as if a heavy bird had landed on my shoulder and leaned down to bury its beak in my side. I was so tired I thought I would never move again. Then from your room came a faint whimpering and at once I was on my feet, hurrying to be there as you woke.

At first the bird came so seldom, and stayed so briefly, that it was easy to ignore. By the time you reached thirty inches on the bath-room door, its visits were more frequent. I would have to come in from the clothesline, or leave the potatoes half peeled, and sit down until it flew away. On the morning of your second birthday I woke with a cry at 4 A.M. and spent the rest of the night pacing the living room.

I spoke of this to no one, not Matthew, not Anne, not the companions, until Dr. Singer, calling unexpectedly, caught me on the sofa in the middle of the day and asked what was wrong.

"Nothing. I just felt a little tired." I sat up with an attempt at briskness. "Let me put the kettle on."

"No, wait. You've been tired a lot recently."

Sentence by sentence, he persuaded me to reveal my symptoms. As I spoke, he balanced on the edge of a chair; his hair, newly cut, bristled boyishly. "You must come and see me," he said.

"That's silly." I rose to my feet. "I'm not really ill and you're so busy."

"I have an opening at three o'clock on Thursday. You can get the school bus. Bring Ruth. My wife would love to see her." He told me to sit down again and went to make the tea.

I did not mention the appointment to Matthew beforehand, nor did I tell him afterwards that, although Dr. Singer could find nothing wrong, he was sending me to Perth for a more thorough examination. There was now a weekly bus from the school into town, and three weeks later we caught it. You enjoyed the journey, pressing your nose to the window and pointing to each passing car. But as soon as we reached the infirmary, you began to scream and would not be quieted.

"Dear me," said the doctor, "somebody's upset." He dangled his stethoscope playfully before you. You paused, only to draw breath. "You'd better take her away," he told the nurse.

The nurse, a spindly girl, carried you from the room at arm's length, as if she had never held a child before. From the hall your cries continued, unabated.

"Now, Mrs. Livingstone, what can I do for you?"

The urge to rescue you was so strong I had to hold on to the chair, but I did my best to describe the pain. The doctor scribbled a couple of lines, then asked me to undress to my underwear and put on a gown. He left the room. A few minutes later he returned, accompanied by the spindly nurse. He pressed my stomach and abdomen. Does it hurt here? he asked. Does this hurt?

All I could think was: Where is Ruth? Who is holding her now? I answered his questions as shortly as possible. The pain was diffuse. I was tired. The doctor shone lights in my eyes, listened to my chest.

"Everything seems normal," he said. "I suspect a touch of indigestion. I'd recommend a daily dose of Epsom salts. Don't eat after eight at night." He patted my shoulder. "Nothing the matter with you, my girl, that a little country air won't cure."

There was another piercing shriek. "Thank you, doctor." Still in my patient's gown, I hurried to retrieve you, red-faced and distraught, from the arms of a strange nurse.

On the bus home, we took the seat in front of the Plishkas; you turned around to talk. Mrs. Plishka, as usual, had her knitting, and as we passed Huntingtower she unwound a piece of wool to make a cat's cradle. "Look, Ruth," she said.

I watched you pluck the wool with your small hands, and a wave of homesickness swept over me. I longed to have Lily tuck me into bed and stand over me with a cup of nettle tea. Then David would come to tell me stories about Barbara and the Pictish chieftains and the giant. "We're lucky," he would insist. "We must share what we have." I leaned my forehead against the seat in front and wished I had never agreed to Dr. Singer's suggestion.

Next day when he called in, I repeated the doctor's comment. "Indigestion? Nonsense. Listen, we'll get you an appointment with the consultant. He'll be at the infirmary in January."

I would have declined if I had not recognised the consultant's name. Sir Hamilton practised in Edinburgh, but he had sometimes been summoned to Glasgow for problematic cases. He was rumoured to be infallible when it came to diagnosis. At once I became hopeful. I imagined him saying, "Mrs. Livingstone, you have . . . We'll soon fix that." He would order a prescription, or even a minor operation, and I would be well again.

After Dr. Singer left, I went out to the kitchen to make supper. There was nothing in the larder but eggs, potatoes, and a pork pie. I was regarding the last dubiously—perhaps it would do for Matthew—when I heard you say, "You're too big." In the living room I found you kneeling beside the fort you'd built. The girl was sitting in the armchair, smiling.

"Who are you talking to?" I asked.

"Johnnie." You held up your stuffed elephant, brown corduroy with blue trousers.

The girl, still smiling, raised her empty hands.

Autumn advanced. The house grew dirtier and meals more perfunctory, but Matthew seemed to notice nothing. Only major omissions, like the complete absence of clean shirts on a Sunday when he had to read the lesson, registered. In the mornings I got up to make his breakfast and, after he had left, returned to bed with you. For a while you listened happily to stories about Percy, the bad chick, and Mrs. Tiggywinkle. Then you grew restless. "Let's get up," you said. "Let's get up and play."

When I acceded to your demands, I would find the house occupied by the companions. All day long they pressed in with terrible eagerness. On Friday they grew dismal at the prospect of Matthew's presence; on Monday, as soon as he left to teach, they reappeared. And, as in the months before your birth, they became surprisingly helpful. When we moved we had bought a washing machine, and in the last year I had trained Matthew to fill the coal scuttles. Still, that left many chores, and the companions began to make the beds, pick up your toys, hang out the nappies. Unfortunately they did not care for fire or water or sharp knives, and they detested the odour of cleaning products.

Once or twice, when the pain was at its worst, I caught them watching me with the same gravity I had glimpsed on the woman's face at your christening. But the tradition of silence still held between us. Do not ask, their eyes said.

One of my first patients in Glasgow, a former missionary to China, had described being in an earthquake. There's this awful moment, he said, when everything you take for granted begins to shake. And that is how I think of the events that occurred a few weeks after our trip to the infirmary. You were asleep in your cot. I was sitting in the living room, trying to darn Matthew's socks and chatting to the woman. She was perched on a stool by the hearth. "Guess what I heard Ruth say this morning," she said. "'What a palaver!'"

"It's an expression of Matthew's. She has no idea what it means, but she knows we think it's funny. She says, 'Goodness gracious,' too. And 'dearie me.'"

The woman was laughing as the door swung open and Anne came in with Robert. Our conversation had masked the sounds of her arrival. "Oh," she said. "I didn't know you had company."

I jumped up, dropping the sock. "Anne." I hurried towards her, took her hand, and drew her out of the room.

In the corridor I stopped, trembling, stupefied. I could not think of a single thing to say. Just as Anne spoke—she asked what was the matter—tears saved me. I sobbed with noisy abandon until first Robert, then you, joined in.

"Hush, hush," said Anne ineffectually, to the three of us.

In all this confusion there was no time for questions. At last my sobs died down and I tried to appease you; Anne did the same for Robert. Only when we returned to the living room with tea and sandwiches to find it empty, did she ask what had become of my visitor.

"She had to go," I said. "She left while you were getting Ruth from her room." I bent to tie on your bib. My mind was racing, searching for a plausible explanation. Someone from the infirmary? No. Someone asking for directions? But a stranger wouldn't sit by the hearth. A friend of Lily's, that was it, who happened to be staying at the Fulford Inn.

While Anne poured us tea and busied herself with Robert, I invented Mrs. Watson, on her way to Blairgowrie. How long is she staying? Anne asked. Just tonight, I said. Oh, said Anne, that's a pity. She looked nice.

Thankfully, it was time for *Twenty Questions* on the wireless, and we could both pretend to listen.

✦══○

Matthew was easy to deceive and Anne was intimidated by my sub-
terfuges, but you knew neither deception nor intimidation. You
could walk easily, and all through the summer you had complained
whenever I picked you up. Now, as the days grew shorter, you demanded to be carried with increasing frequency. "Carry me," you
were saying, "not the pain."

In early December, nearly a fortnight after Anne had seen the
woman, she and I took Robert and you to play on the swing that
hung from the cooper beech beside the Grange. As we trundled up
with our prams, the sound of barking came from the house. "Dogs,"
you said hopefully, but no dogs appeared.

The ground beneath the tree was thick with leaves. While Anne
pushed Robert, you bent to examine them, and I remembered the
churchyard in Troon, the dead leaves drifting over Barbara's grave.
Next summer, I thought, we should go for a holiday. Lily would
come too, and we could stay at the Bell and Bush, visit Ballintyre,
and play on the beach.

Robert had soon had enough of the swing, but you clamoured
for turn after turn. Finally I said, "I'm sorry, darling. I'm too tired."

"I'll give you a turn," said Anne.

Your lips quivered. "No. I want Mummy. I want a turn with
Mummy."

"What a silly girl you are." In spite of the darkness that rose
around me, I hoisted you onto the swing and pushed you back and
forth until Anne called a halt. Before you could protest, she had you
seated in the pram. We started up the hill towards home. As we

reached the California redwood, Anne said, "Eva, I don't mean to pry but are you all right?"

I steered the pram around a pothole left by the autumn rain. I could feel Anne watching me and I knew she saw what Matthew did not: how thin I'd grown, how pale. Since the afternoon she'd surprised me with the woman, there had been a wariness between us. Sadly, I thought she must attribute my odd behaviour to some failure of affection. Now, in an effort to recover our closeness, I told her about the appointment with Sir Hamilton.

"Oh, good," she said. "At last you're being sensible. I can look after Ruth. You know I'm always happy to have her."

That evening as I sang you to sleep, I wondered for the hundredth time why someone else had finally glimpsed a companion. Anne was a dear friend, but other dear friends—Isobel, Daphne, Samuel—had seen only empty air. I recalled my last meeting with Neal Cunningham. I could still picture his face, blackened with tannic acid, and the jovial smile of his companion as he bore Neal away, briskly, in a wheelchair, to his death.

I shivered, and at the same moment a tremor passed over you, like wind over a field. I reached down to stroke your back. I wanted to shield you from every harm and danger.

18

At night I waited until Matthew was asleep, then I slipped from our bed to pace the quiet rooms, hoping that fatigue would overcome pain. I longed for the opiates I had given to others, but why should I have drugs for an illness with no name? Often the woman came to share my vigils. She plied me with questions. Had you learned to sing "Away in a Manger"? Was Matthew still busy with exams? Would Lily come for Christmas? Had I heard that people were once again planning holidays in France? One night, when the pain was especially acute and frost flowered the windows, a feeling of recklessness came over me. "Why me?" I said.

"What do you mean?"

"Why do you visit me? Why do you take care of me?"

For a moment she looked dumbfounded, and I thought she would do what she always did in the face of awkward questions:

vanish. She stared down at her moss-green skirt, pleating the material back and forth between her fingers. "Do you remember how you used to think of us like a flash of colour or a note of music?"

"Blue and silver, D sharp and middle C."

"Well, that's not far from the truth. Our natures can't be spoken, even by us. Why some of us come back and some do not, I don't know, anymore than you know why you usually overcook the potatoes." She raised her eyes to mine. "I do know that only a few people can give us life, people who have lost someone at a young age. We cling to them."

"And do I have a say?"

"Oh"—she leaned forward eagerly—"it all depends on you. When Samuel asked you to give us up, you could have."

I sank down into the armchair. "So he was right."

The woman nodded. "We behaved unfortunately. We knew you liked him, so we tried to help. Then it became apparent that Samuel was like a cuckoo; he wanted to push us out of the nest. But it all depended on you."

I eyed her raptly, everything else forgotten. "And Matthew? You even took him to the shop to buy the ring."

"Matthew is different. Besides, you wanted a child."

So did you, I nearly added, but I hurried on. "The girl is Barbara's sister, Elizabeth. Who are you?"

"Marion Hanscombe. Your mother saved my son's life. When I helped you lift David from the river, I was doing no more than she had done." She smiled. "And the man who came to cheer you up? You were right; that was Barbara's uncle Jack."

"So why doesn't Barbara come? Why you three and not her?"

"I've wondered that too. Maybe she was missed so much, there was no need for her to return. In a way, she never left." Her smile faded. "You should get some rest." Before I could reply, she was gone.

Alone in the empty room I glimpsed the last exit in a dark maze—the maze which I had all unwittingly entered, years before, beneath the red-currant bushes—and dreaded the illumination I might find. I padded down the corridor to kneel beside your bed. Everything else might be in question, but you, your sweet breath, was real. Suddenly I realised the pain had dipped below the horizon. I hurried back to bed and slept.

On the day of my appointment with Sir Hamilton, Anne insisted that I ask Matthew to drive me to Perth. I hated to alarm him, but I need not have worried. He fussed briefly and then, taking my word that it was a routine checkup, began to look forward to an afternoon in town. When we arrived at the infirmary he said, "Can I just drop you? I thought I might pop into Deucars to see his new books."

On my last few visits I had bypassed the infirmary waiting room. Now I had ample time to take in the dingy decor: blackout blinds still hung in the windows, and on the wall was a LOOSE LIPS SINK SHIPS poster. A dozen other people were already gathered, and as I took my seat I studied them curiously. Beside me a dapper middle-aged couple—the man in a checked suit, the woman in a well-cut dress—were talking quietly. Next to them a man and a small boy with his arm in a sling read a comic. Near the door two women, sisters perhaps, were knitting. Everyone, except the boy, appeared to be in good health, and somehow this made me feel better—we all had hidden illnesses.

At last the nurse called my name. I followed her across the corridor into a consulting room. Sir Hamilton was seated at a table, with a small group of interns standing deferentially behind him. He was reading a file, mine I presumed, and all I could see was the crown of his head, white and bony through the thinning hair.

No one spoke. In the silence I found myself remembering Samuel and how good he had been at putting his patients at ease. Then Sir Hamilton raised his head and I felt the weight of his brisk scrutiny. "So, Mrs. Livingstone, you have a pain. I've read the reports of my colleagues and there's nothing very illuminating. Could you describe it for me?"

"I have a pain in the abdominal region. It fluctuates in intensity and seems unrelated to diet or exercise. Occasionally it causes nausea."

"Were you a nurse?"

"Yes, sir. Glasgow Infirmary 1939–45."

"Good, good. I see Dr. Singer ordered some X rays. Why don't we start by taking a look at those?"

A nurse put two X rays up on the screen. Sir Hamilton and the doctors gathered round. From where I sat I could hear him, ticking off my organs. "I must say," he said at last, "everything looks fine, but as you're here I may as well examine you."

I went into the examination room and changed into a gown. For two pins I would have turned and fled, but I thought of Dr. Singer, who had worked hard to get me this appointment, and I thought of you. I lay down and waited. Presently Sir Hamilton came in, entourage at his heels. He lifted the gown and began to palpate me. "Does this hurt?" he asked. "Does this?"

I answered wearily. It all hurt, no one place more than another.

"Well, Mrs. Livingstone, you seem fit as a fiddle. I see in your file you date your illness to the birth of your child. Unfortunately many women do allow childbirth to turn them into hypochondriacs."

Behind him the interns nodded, a jury echoing a judge. I remembered Daphne sneering at the private patients with their nerves and hernias. I remembered Sir William, the hospital ghost, taunting the young man with headaches. "I'm sorry," I stammered. "Perhaps I have a touch of indigestion."

But Sir Hamilton was already leaving the room. Only one of the interns lingered, a stocky young man whose white coat barely buttoned around him. "Have you always been this thin?" he asked.

"Just since my daughter was born."

"These X rays don't show everything. Ask your doctor to get a complete set." He hurried away.

In the waiting room, Matthew dropped the newspaper and stood to meet me. "Eva." He put his hands on my shoulders. "Are you all right?"

Through my dress I felt his touch, warm and sure, and for a moment I wanted to throw myself into his arms. I had to swallow before I could repeat Sir Hamilton's verdict.

"Splendid," he said. And suddenly, seeing his face break into a smile, I understood that my uncertain health had not entirely passed him by. He bent to kiss me.

Back at Glenaird we went straight to collect you. Anne invited us in for tea, but I said it was your bedtime. I wanted to avoid her anxious sympathy and in particular the need to tell her that it was unjustified. As we drove up the hill, I asked about your afternoon. "We painted," you said. "And we made biscuits."

We turned off the main road. "Look," you exclaimed. In your

excitement you almost slipped from my arms. In the headlights of the car a group of black-and-white birds were strutting up and down in front of the house.

"Magpies," said Matthew. "Can you count them, Ruth?"

"One, two," you called, pointing wildly. "Three."

"Four, five," he prompted.

"Six," you said triumphantly. The birds rose as one and flew off into the darkness.

That night after Matthew had fallen asleep, I got out of bed. I went into the living room and switched on the overhead light and all three lamps. Marian and Elizabeth were on the sofa, as if they had been waiting for me. The man with a moustache, Barbara's uncle Jack, stood against the wall, and beside him the soldiers from the river.

I did my best to ignore them. All my life, I thought, I had been too credulous. I had believed in the companions and that belief gave them power. Now it was the same with my illness. *"Malade imaginaire,"* I murmured. If I could only rid myself of this foolish notion, then I would be well again.

I began to pick up your toys. Even that slight exertion exhausted me, but I forced myself to go on. "There's nothing the matter with me," I whispered grimly. When I finished, I looked around the room. The desk caught my attention. I had never liked it by the window. How much larger the room would seem if it were in the corner.

The desk had two pedestals and twenty pigeonholes; two men had carried it into the house with considerable effort; Lily and I had tried in vain to lift it. If I can move this, I thought, the pain will vanish. I grasped a corner. "One, two, three." I heaved. I might as well have tried to push back the walls.

I stopped to reconsider. My heart was pounding, as if my blood had thickened and could only with huge effort be forced through my veins. I wiped the hair from my forehead and took a tentative step forward. Beneath my feet the floor buckled. I closed my eyes and waited for it to grow flat.

When I looked up again, Marian and Elizabeth were beside me. Elizabeth touched my arm, motioning towards the sofa. Her face was much paler than usual; her eight freckles stood out, tiny and distinct. I shook my head and turned back to my task.

Marian barred my way. Against her dark dress her hair shone like snow on a winter's morning. "Excuse me," I said. "I'm moving the desk."

"Please, Eva. Sit down and rest."

In her deep-set, melting grey eyes I seemed to see all those occasions when the companions had come to my aid: They had saved me from the gypsies, they had persuaded Lily to let me go to the infirmary, they had rescued me after the air raid. I saw the men in uniform lift David out of the river and carry him to safety. They had brought me to Matthew, and to you.

Slowly I turned my head to break her gaze. Then I did what I had never done before. I stepped blindly forward as if she did not exist.

19

I was not surprised to open my eyes and see the green screens around my bed. From the familiar odour that greeted my first conscious breath, I had known I was in a hospital. But where were you? In my fear I tried to get up, but the normal link between impulse and action was broken. I was as helpless as if bound to the bed. Even to crook my little finger was an effort.

Then I thought Anne would be taking care of you; it was better for you not to see me like this. I lay back, hoping someone would come. On the ceiling two roughly triangular cracks resembled the shaky maps of Africa and India I had drawn as a child. I stared at them, trying to recall the different countries, the spice routes.

At last a nurse appeared between the screens. She had dark hair, and for a confused moment I mistook her for Daphne. Oh, she'd soon have me well. "How are you feeling, Mrs. Livingstone?"

I shaped a response, but no words emerged. I held on to the nurse's sleeve. Up close she was nothing like Daphne. Her hair was straight and no one would have accused her for a moment of using makeup. After a minute I managed to whisper, "Where am I?"

"Newcastle Infirmary. They brought you in last night."

"Newcastle." Fear gave me the strength to speak louder. "Could you get the sister?"

She disappeared and I lay with my heart struggling in my chest. How could I be in Newcastle and not know it? Where were you?

The sister bent over me, her face large as the moon. "Good morning, Mrs. Livingstone, this must be very confusing. You collapsed, and your husband arranged for you to be brought here to Newcastle Infirmary so that you could be under the care of Dr. Halliday, an old friend of his."

"Where is my daughter?"

"Your husband is in the waiting room. We don't normally allow visitors now but I'll have him fetched. He'll explain."

A few minutes later Matthew tiptoed towards the bed. He was unshaven and his collar and cuffs were edged with grime. I recognised the maroon tie you had given him for Christmas. "Eva," he murmured, "thank God." He sank down on the edge of the bed and took my hands in his.

I felt my eyes fill with tears as I waited for news of you.

"I woke up," he said, "and you were gone." Although this often happened, for some reason he had been alarmed and had got up at once. He had found me lying on the living room floor with you curled beside me. "At first I thought you were both asleep," Matthew said, "but I couldn't rouse you. Ruth woke and I told her I was going out for a few minutes.

"I rushed from the house and drove to Anne's. She was wonderful. She sent Paul to telephone Dr. Singer, then she came immediately. When we got back, Ruth was having a sort of fit. She was shaking you and shouting, 'Mummy, wake up! Mummy, come back!'

"Dr. Singer arrived and said you were unconscious. While we were waiting for the ambulance, I telephoned Tink Halliday and he suggested we bring you down here."

"What about Ruth?"

"Ruth is fine. She's with Anne."

"Can I see her?"

"When you're better, darling. It would only upset her to bring her here. Besides, what would I do with her? I'm staying in a lodging house just round the corner."

"Please, Matthew. I want her to know that I'm all right."

He shifted his chair and cleared his throat. "Why don't we wait until Tink has examined you? Then we'll make plans. He's coming to see you as soon as he's finished his rounds." Matthew smiled. "He's a wonderful doctor, Eva. He used to practise in Stoke-on-Trent. I remember when the fishmonger's boy was run over by a cart. Everyone said he'd lose his legs, but Tink had him walking in less than a year. And there was a woman——"

"I'll have to ask you to leave, sir. We're doing the beds."

The nurses lifted me briskly from side to side, talking as if I were still unconscious. "The carrots are always soggy," the taller one said, stretching the bottom sheet.

"And cabbage three times a week. Can you move her a bit higher?"

When they had gone, I sank back against the clean sheets. The image of you trying to wake me was unbearable. But Anne would look after you, I thought, and perhaps at long last the doctors would discover what was wrong. They would operate and I would be cured. I remembered how ill Scott had been; he had recovered.

Comforted, I allowed my eyes to close. But before I could fall asleep, the pain began to rise. Since I woke it had been flickering dully. Now it twisted into my side, sharp and fierce, as it had when I tried to move the desk. Escape was impossible.

When Dr. Halliday came, the first thing he did was give me an injection. He stood beside the bed, a small neat-featured man, watching until he saw from my eyes that the morphine was taking effect. "So, Eva, I hear you've been poorly. We'll soon have you back on your feet."

"Do you know what's wrong?"

"We did some tests while you were unconscious," he said. "We should have the results in a few days."

"And then you'll operate," I whispered.

"Operate." He seemed to be examining his stethoscope. "Why would we operate? Nothing the matter with you that a little rest won't cure."

The initial rush of the morphine had died down, and in its wake I understood my predicament. I knew, as surely as if Dr. Halliday had told me, that there was no hope. My body had been occupied by an invisible enemy. If they would not operate, then already it was too late. I gazed at Dr. Halliday until reluctantly he raised his eyes to mine. In them I saw the words he could not say. He patted my hand and turned away.

During the days that followed I forgot night and day. The hours were marked not by the sun but by the course of the pain. It rose swift and unassailable, and each attack I thought must be the zenith would prove to be a mere foreshadowing. Then an injection would come and for a few hours I could think of you.

I pictured myself back at Rookery Nook. You were kneeling on the living room floor, building a house for Johnnie, your elephant. Your face was fierce with concentration as you reached for the next brick. I remembered the morning of your birth, when Matthew and I had walked up and down the road in our nightclothes. If I were strong enough, I thought, I would walk from Newcastle to Glenaird. I imagined myself putting one foot in front of the other on the long smooth roads until at last I came up over the rise in the road where Matthew had proposed and down into the valley which I now knew as home.

Every time he came to see me, I asked for you. "Darling," he said, "can't you wait a few weeks? You'll be better and the three of us will take a holiday. Your first visit to England. You mustn't spend it all lying in bed." He laughed at his feeble joke. Then he read Lily's daily letter. Soon after I arrived in Newcastle, she had come to take care of you.

> *Ruth and I are managing fine. I've discovered the hard way that she detests mince and can only take a bath if Johnnie is watching. We're both looking forward to seeing you very soon.*

I smiled faintly. It gave me pleasure to think of Lily doing with you the things she had once done with me.

⇥

I woke in darkness to the voices of two women talking beyond the screens that always seemed to surround my bed. For a moment I wondered if the companions had come.

"How is she?" one said.

"It's a miracle she's still alive," said the other. "The cancer's spread from the liver to the pancreas. No one thought she'd hang on this long."

"Poor thing. You know she has a daughter?"

"That must be the Ruth she's always talking about. And Mrs. Murphy?"

As soon as the women mentioned you, I knew they were nurses; the companions would never speak of you that way. It was possible, I thought, that Mrs. Hanscombe and Elizabeth would never come again. I was not entirely sure what had happened the night I tried to move the desk, but dimly I recalled I had betrayed them.

In bits and pieces the nurses' remarks came back. Cancer. The word was as well-worn as the stones Ian had taught me to skip over the water. It had been there all along, nestling on the pillow, waiting to be picked up. Beyond grief or despair, I felt momentarily a sense of vindication. I was not a hypochondriac.

Then I understood the gravity of my situation. I had allowed myself to be lulled by Matthew's optimism, by the intermittent peace of the injections, into forgetting what Dr. Halliday had inadvertently told me. The only time to see you was now. In the hours that followed I held fast to this thought.

It was barely light when Matthew appeared. As he launched into his customary remarks—"The landlady served fried bread"—I summoned all my energy.

"Matthew," I interrupted. "I heard the nurses talking last night. I'm not going to get well." I spoke deliberately in the same simple sentences that I used when explaining to you how to tie your shoelaces. "Please ask Lily to bring Ruth. I have to see her. Before it's too late."

"Nonsense, Eva." He paused to clear his throat. "You're on the mend. Dr. Halliday is positive you'll be fine by spring."

"Please," I said.

But he had already begun his litany about my recovery, the famous holiday. We would go to Troon and I would show you both my home. "We'll splurge," he said, "and stay in the best hotel. No expense spared."

His lips were trembling. He knows, I thought, and briefly I longed to comfort him.

Then visiting hours were over. Matthew bent to kiss me, and in his place a nurse appeared. Before I could grasp what was happening, the needle slid into my arm. "You'll feel better now," she said. I recognised her voice. She was one of the two whom I had heard talking in the dark. Then I remembered you, Ruth. Before I could follow the thought further, the morphine carried me away, far out of reach of words or deeds.

That night I woke to find Marian Hanscombe sitting by my bed. Standing behind her was Elizabeth. I was overjoyed. I tried to utter the words of apology that had been running through my mind for days. No sound came, but Marian seemed to understand. She stroked my forehead, and her touch made me feel clear and calm. "My dear," she said, "don't worry about us. You owe us nothing. It's we who owe you. We've come now to pay our debt."

"Did you know I was ill?" I whispered.

"We've known all along. There was nothing we could do. Nothing anyone could do."

Again I tried to speak, but Marian's hand soothed away the need for questions and answers. "Listen, we're going to take you to Ruth. She's expecting you. Close your eyes."

I let my eyes fall shut. I felt Marian kiss my cheek and then Elizabeth. The sheets and blankets fell away as they lifted me from the bed. There was a rush of warm air and a faint prickling sensation, like the falling of dew on a summer evening.

"Open your eyes," said Marian. "Don't be afraid."

I was standing in the doorway of your room. The night-light burned on the table, and I could see you asleep in bed with your doll beside you. I took a step forward but Marian held me back. "Will you do something for us?" she asked.

"Anything."

"Tell Ruth we're here. We need her."

I nodded, all opposition ironed away in the heat of my desire for you. And yet, between one breath and the next, I remembered and took comfort in what Marian had told me, that I myself had chosen the companions. I could have sent them away. You too, I thought, would make your choice.

They helped me walk to the bed. As we drew near, you woke. "Mummy," you exclaimed.

You climbed out of bed and ran to me, arms outstretched. I

stepped away from the companions. I found the strength to lift you up. I kissed your forehead and your cheeks and the warm crease in your neck.

"I built a fort for us," you said.

I raised my head and saw at the foot of the bed a circle of bricks and pillows. "What a big fort," I said. "It looks very strong."

I carried you over and stepped inside. Something soft brushed my foot. Looking down, I saw your stuffed elephant propped against a cushion. "You brought Johnnie."

"So he'll be safe." You tightened your arms round my neck.

Marian and Elizabeth retreated to the doorway. Slowly I knelt down. I stroked your hair where it stuck up in little tufts. "I'm sorry I went away," I said.

You pursed your lips. "Promise you won't go away again."

For a moment I closed my eyes. Then I opened them and drew back slightly so as to look into your face. Matthew was right; you do have Elizabeth's dark eyebrows and high forehead, and I think you have her sense of mischief. "I promise, but you may not always know that I'm keeping my promise." I kissed your forehead. "Now it's the middle of the night. You have to go back to sleep."

"Tell me a story."

"I know a good story," I said. "Once upon a time there was a girl called Elizabeth. She was your grandmother's sister. She had very long pigtails and she knew the names of all the birds and flowers. When she was fourteen she caught polio and died. But she came back to take care of her sister, and then of me. She used to play with me when I was a little girl. If you want her to, she'll play with you too."

You yawned and buried your head in my chest.

"Years after Elizabeth died, your grandmother was walking by the sea when a boy fell into the water. She rescued him, and his mother, Mrs. Hanscombe, became her friend. Mrs. Hanscombe has been my best friend, too. She has silver hair and speaks excellent French. It's because of her that I came to Glenaird and married your father and you were born."

I felt you sliding into sleep, and myself sliding into something deeper and longer. I looked across the room. Marian and Elizabeth were smiling. Then I saw a third figure, the companions' final gift.

Barbara stepped forward, lightly, as if she were humming a song under her breath. Her long blue dress rustled like autumn leaves and her brown hair was pinned, untidily, into a bun. She wore the circular spectacles that had reduced her to tears at the optician's and made David try to comfort her. She crossed the room, and when she reached the fort she held out her hand.

Without letting go of you, I took my mother's hand. I found myself gazing into the face I had always known. Barbara smiled at me with gentle gaiety. "Eva, I've been waiting for you."

"I don't want to leave Ruth."

"You won't," said Barbara. "What you told her is true. You'll never leave her." She gave the slightest pull to my hand.

By this time you were sleeping steadfastly. I kissed your cheek and whispered in your ear again the promise I had just made. Then I laid you down beside your animals and stepped out of the fort into Barbara's arms.

As we embraced, I realised I was several inches taller than her. No wonder her wedding dress had been too small. My cheek lay against Barbara's hair and I breathed in a faint bitter tang. It must, I thought, be the odour of explosives.

I was buried in the village churchyard on the first day of February in a plot next to my grandparents and Elizabeth. As the school's bachelor masters carried the coffin across the churchyard, a flock of small birds rose, twittering, from the branches of the yew tree. Sleet fell from the dark sky upon the heads of the mourners and into the open grave.

Only three people had come to my christening. Many times that number came to my funeral. Scott was crying. Mrs. Thornton had her handkerchief to her face. Matthew stood motionless between Lily and Anne; throughout the brief ceremony his gaze never left the coffin. Only the person upon whom I had turned all my last thoughts was not present that day. You were with the first of many strangers. Anne had brought a bunch of violets on your behalf, and when the coffin was lowered into the grave, she stepped forward and placed the small purple flowers upon the shining wood. I have them still.

ACKNOWLEDGEMENTS

A novel written over a decade incurs many obligations. My apologies if any, in the fullness of time, have been forgotten.

In my reading about the Second World War, two books were particularly helpful: *A Nurse's War,* by Brenda McBryde, and *Faces from the Fire,* by Leonard Moseley. Those familiar with the latter will recognise that Samuel Rosenblum is loosely based on the legendary plastic surgeon Archie McIndoe, head of the famous burns unit at East Grinstead.

Although this novel is set in Scotland, I have taken certain liberties with the landscape. My versions of Troon and Glasgow cannot be mapped exactly onto those real places.

I am grateful to Amanda Urban, who believed that this book could see the light of day, and to Jennifer Barth, John Sterling, and the other wonderful people at Henry Holt for making that possible.

ACKNOWLEDGEMENTS

Various friends commented on the manuscript and encouraged me, perhaps unwittingly, to keep going. My thanks to Tom Bahr, Charles Baxter, Robert Boswell, Carol Frost, Eddy Harris, Jim Shepard, Chuck Wachtel.

To those who understood that the life and the work were intertwined and who helped me to live the former and write the latter, I owe a special debt: Eric Garnick, Kathleen Hill, Camille Smith, Holly Zeeb. To Susan Brison, whose friendship has happily sustained me for twenty-five years, I offer my deep thanks.

The story began with Merril and Roger Sylvester on a Scottish hillside. Andrea Barrett helped me to finish it.

This book is for Eva Barbara Malcolm McEwen, whose short life I regret making, in the interests of fiction, still shorter.

About the Author

MARGOT LIVESEY is the award-winning author of a story collection, *Learning by Heart,* and the novels *Homework, Criminals,* and *The Missing World*. She grew up in Scotland and currently lives and teaches in the Boston area.